Acknowledgments

This book would not be complete without my editor, Adam Cooper. Thanks for all the time and effort you put into my book.

A special thanks to all of the people who donated to my GoFundMe campaign. Justin May, Maleah Thompson, Melody Barnette, Tina Korossy, Tammie Lanham, Michael Myers, and Adam Cooper.

My author photograph was taken by the talented Samantha Page McNease.

Brad Collier, thanks for putting up with my craziness for the past couple of years!

To my amazing mother,
Thanks for being the light in the dark, strength when I'm
weak, and my twin!

Broken Arrow

Prologue

This world is not a place that embraces being different. Society asks everyone to fit into a mold. People's lights are dimmed all because others are not comfortable. It's a tough journey for anyone who tries to let their light shine through the darkness of this difficult existence. However, making it through is what life is all about.

On September 18th, 1997, Max Stevenson was born in Sandersville, Kentucky. His mother, barely prepared, decided to keep him. He was an accident that turned into a miracle. He was the reason his parents got married. It was because of him that his family was formed.

Right from the start, Max's parents had plans for their sweet baby boy. His mom wanted him to be a doctor, nurse, dentist, or anything else in the health industry because she knew those kinds of jobs made good money. His dad wanted him to find a nice woman, get married, and settle down with kids. They pushed their idea of a perfect life onto their son. He had no input in the matter.

Expectations can be a dangerous thing. They have the

power to set someone up for painful disappointment. When you place expectations on a child, you put both yourself and the child at risk of feeling the weight of failure. Max wasn't born into a time that would embrace who he was. He was born into a world that made him an outcast. Max was placed on the battleground of a brutal and painful mental war.

The heat of expectations cooled down when Cole Stevenson was born. He was Max's beautiful baby brother. He strengthened the Stevenson family's bond. Max began to wonder how he ever survived being an only child. Cole made everything complete for them. They were a perfect little family.

It only takes one disruption to turn perfection into utter chaos. Peace can be interrupted in an instant. The truth always finds a way to get out, and sometimes that truth is more than some minds can handle. The fact that Max was gay had the power to change everything.

Chapter 1

"I'm gay!" Max Stevenson said with sweat pouring down his pale, round face. He looked around the dinner table and tried to read everyone's facial expressions. Everything went dead quiet. You could hear his husky, Cooper, slurping water from his bowl. This went on for what felt like five minutes to Max. He had to remind himself to breathe before his mother finally spoke up.

"Honey, I'm glad you told us!" his mom, Natalie, said with a loving voice. "You know we still love you. That will never change." Natalie was beautiful and blonde with a short pixie haircut. She was always very liberal. She worked at the front desk of a local hotel.

Max exhaled a huge sigh of relief. The person he felt closest to still loved him for who he was. Honestly, he wasn't surprised by her reaction. From what he knew from the past, his mom didn't seem to have a problem with the LGBTQ (Lesbian, Gay, Bisexual, Transgender, and Questioning) community. He knew he was on his way to a better life after his mom spoke those words to him, but as

Max knew all too well, not everything could always be perfect.

"I don't understand, Max." Greg, his father, broke his silence. "Why would you want to choose this lifestyle for yourself? There's so much you're giving up!" Greg's black hair was starting to turn gray from the stress he already had to deal with while working at a local car dealership. He always had a stern, scruffy face. He was the definition of a business man.

Max's mom gave her husband a look that told Max he shouldn't let his father's words get to him. Still, Max's heart dropped to his stomach. He wasn't emotionally strong enough to argue back against his dad's opinions. He was paralyzed in his seat as he hoped for a way out of the moment. Was coming out really the best idea? Max was already past the point of no return.

"So, you like other boys?" A young voice saved the day. Cole was Max's ten-year-old brother. One of the most curious kids Max knew, Cole had light brown hair that went down to his shoulders. His narrow face seemed intrigued by Max's news.

Max's mom helped explain the situation to Cole while his dad sat quietly with a bothered look on his face. For once, Max didn't feel like the outcast in the room. He could see that his father was the outcast this time. As happy as Max was to not feel like the odd one out, he still felt bad for his father. Max wanted to be close to him, but their only common ground was religion, which was now a sore topic for Max. All hope of having a good father-son relationship now seemed lost.

Max knew he had sacrificed a lot of time to try and be close to his father. He believed that one of the worst feelings in life was to work really hard on something just to see it fall apart. There was nothing more Max could do to help the relationship from his perspective. It was up to his dad to make some effort to keep their relationship alive.

After dinner, Max went to his room to clear his head. He couldn't help but wonder what his dad really thought of him now. He began to get a little stressed thinking about the disappointment on his dad's face. He turned on Chase Coy, his favorite acoustic singer, and began writing in his journal.

I actually did it! I came out to my family! After 18 long years in the dark and gloomy closet, I have stepped into the light. Overall, it went better than I thought it would. Of course, Dad wasn't thrilled. Shocker! I'm happy Mom helped me explain things to Cole. I wouldn't know what to say to him.

The best part about all of this is the fact that I can say goodbye to the dark cloud known as depression. I grew up hating myself because I was gay. It didn't help that Dad made us all go to church every week. That's where I learned to hate myself even though I tried loving myself there. It took me such a long time to come to terms with the fact that I was gay. When I finally did, I remained depressed because nobody really knew who I was. Now, I can start to tell everyone in my life the truth and be free of my sadness once and for all!

Suddenly, Max heard a knock on his door. His mom creaked the door open, and Max told her it was okay for her to come in. His mom sat down on the bed and began telling

Max how proud she was of him. Max smiled as she continued on talking about how she knew Max was struggling. Max was about to tell her how he knew everything was about to be great when his mom said something that shifted his mood.

"I just want you to understand that this isn't the end of the struggle I know you're dealing with. A lot of the world, your father included, doesn't understand gay people. You're bound to face some adversity," she said with a sincere voice. "And I would be lying to you if I told you I don't think it will bother you. I understand how you feel more than you know. The guilt your upbringing has brought you isn't going to disappear in a day. This is going to be a long journey for you, but I'm always by your side, Max." Natalie kissed her son on the forehead, gave him a smile, and left the room.

Damn! Max lay in bed thinking about the truth bomb his mother just laid on him. Was she right? Max was hoping this was the end of the hardships he had to face. He had always pictured coming out as the finish line. Now, he wondered what was next for him. He spent so much time thinking about this day that he never thought about the aftermath. This wasn't a finish line, it was merely a checkpoint at the beginning of his journey.

Despite his mother's warning, Max only saw happy things when he looked ahead. With nothing to hide, he would be light as a feather. There would be no more stressing over the people who were trying to figure out if he was gay. Also, gay couldn't be used as an insult because it was a truth that Max was no longer ashamed of.

The next day, Max's dad pretended like the previous night had never happened. He ate breakfast with the family then headed off to work. Max hated that he could feel the distance between them. No matter how hard Max fought to not let it bother him, he still wanted his dad to treat him better. He didn't think his dad's behavior was Christian-like at all.

"Have you always been this way?" Cole asked while Max was in the middle of watching Myth Busters on television.

"Yeah, I think so. I just never accepted it until recently." It felt good for Max to be able to talk about his experience.

Cole decided to conduct a full interview with his older brother. Max answered all the questions he could without giving Cole too much information. Max saw his mom standing in the kitchen smiling at the two boys discussing Max's sexuality. Max felt so privileged to have an amazing mother like her.

Max found himself thinking he was more comfortable when his father wasn't in the house. He felt like a horrible son for feeling that way, but it was only because his dad couldn't face the fact that Max was gay. Maybe in time his dad would come around and be able to embrace his oldest son for who he was.

Chapter 2

Five years before coming out...

Max forced himself to eat the chicken patty sandwich on his tray. He knew that it wasn't real chicken, but he had nothing else to eat. Thankfully, the mashed potatoes made up for the disgusting sandwich although nothing could make up for the sadness Max felt sitting alone. A few people would talk to Max, but he didn't have any real friends. He was far too shy to make any social effort.

Being close to his teachers helped him through middle school. They always seemed to care about what Max was feeling which was usually loneliness. His teachers just wanted him to succeed, and he definitely did. He never had a grade lower than a B. He spent a lot of time on homework which was one of the only bonuses to not having friends.

Shock registered visibly on Max's face when he was handed an invitation to his classmate Jamal's birthday party. Jamal wasn't one of the coolest kids in school, but it was Max's first birthday invitation since elementary school. It was even a sleepover. Although Jamal's sense of humor was darker than his skin, Max was excited to go. He RSVP'd right away, even before he asked his parents.

When the bus dropped him off at home that afternoon, he ran in his house and showed his dad the birthday invitation. "Can I go? Can I?" Max asked. He went as far as to get on his knees and beg. He even added a puppy dog pout for good measure.

"Well, go ask your mother. She's making dinner in the kitchen," his father replied, watching as Max ran into the other room.

"Is this one of your friends?" his mom asked him while studying the invitation. She had never heard this kid's name before.

"Of course!" Max lied, hoping she couldn't tell.

Max's mom gave him a look that said she was not convinced, but he was invited so she figured they would be nice to her boy. "Fine, you can go!"

"Yay!" Max began yelling in excitement.

"Hush! Cole is taking a nap on the couch. You know how cranky he gets when he's woken up," his mom said, warning him.

As the week passed, Jamal started talking to Max. Max even got brave enough to go sit with Jamal's group during lunch. He didn't feel like he fit in with them, but at least he wasn't sitting alone. Sitting alone was social suicide. At least now he had the facade that he had close friends.

On the day of the party, Max grabbed his favorite pair of swim trunks and packed clothes for the night. It was a pool party. There would even be a hot tub. Before running out to the car, he grabbed the Captain America action figure he had gotten for Jamal. He jumped in the car then told his mom to hit the gas. He didn't want to be late.

There were so many kids at the party when he arrived. It looked like half the school was there. His mother walked him in and introduced herself to Jamal's mother. Suddenly, everything made sense. Jamal's mother was Mrs. Jackson, another teacher at Sandersville Middle School. Max didn't suspect she was the reason he was invited because he didn't have her as a teacher in class. Yet, that was the only explanation Max could think of.

Max was ecstatic when he was asked to play pool volleyball. He wasn't any good, but he got to interact with the other kids. Eventually his mom got comfortable enough to leave him there alone. She was the mother that stayed the latest. A couple of kids made fun of Max for being a mama's boy, but he tried not to let it get to him. They were just messing around.

Jamal seemed pleased with the gift Max got him. Max had seen him wearing a Captain America shirt at school on occasion. Jamal also got water guns, nerf guns, and a couple of movies. After the gifts were opened, they ate cake. It was absolutely amazing. Max had to admit he was having a better time than he thought he would, considering he wasn't close to anyone.

After Jamal's parents went to bed, all of the boys at the party played board games in Jamal's room. They tried their hardest to learn how to play Risk, but they ended up throwing the pieces at each other. Max sat towards the corner and observed the mayhem. He was too nervous to jump in and join them.

"I have an idea!" Jamal's face looked like he was cooking up an evil plan.

"Pillow fight?" another kid asked.

"No, dummy. This isn't a girl's sleepover. Let's go skinny dip!" he suggested.

Max's throat tightened. Surely Jamal wasn't serious. There would be no way Max could strip down and jump in the pool. He didn't want to be seen naked, but he also didn't want to be seen as a loser. Hopefully it was dark enough that nobody could see anyone else naked.

They all snuck outside, wearing only shorts. Jamal was the first one to take his off. Max forced himself to look away. He'd never seen another boy naked before. He heard others taking off their clothes and getting in the pool.

"Are you coming, Max?" Jamal asked.

"I think I'll just sit out and watch." Max knew he had chosen the wrong choice of words as soon as they left his mouth.

"Watch?!" One boy acted disgusted.

"No! I meant I don't want to get naked! Leave me alone." Max fired back.

Max decided to play *Snake* on his Nokia phone while the other boys goofed around. Part of Max really wanted to join in on the shenanigans, but he didn't want anyone to see his snake. His parents taught him to keep that to himself. After Max beat his own high score, the boys began getting out of the pool.

As a reflex, Max looked up at the boys. A weird tingle ran up his back as he glanced at his first naked boy. This particular boy was thin, and he could see the hint of a six pack. For some reason, Max couldn't look away from the bare body in front of him. He was totally mesmerized.

Max began to feel worried. He had never desired to see a girl naked, but he didn't mind his view of the boys. He never knew why the boys at school talked about hot girls. He never could relate to that. A word that he heard a while back popped in his head. For the first time, Max had to ask himself, "Am I gay?"

Back at school, Max began to hang out by himself again. Eventually Jamal had to move because his mother got another teaching job. Max never forgot that night at the party, but he forced the question of his sexuality to the back of his mind. He assumed it was a phase, so he never gave it a second thought. He would eventually be attracted to women. It was just a matter of time, right?

Chapter 3

Max watched Cole play games on his Xbox as he thought about the fact that Cole was close to the age Max was when he discovered his attraction to boys. Time had passed by so unbelievably fast. Thankfully, Max came out of his shell and gained some friends. Also, he learned to filter what he said so that he would never say he wanted to watch guys skinny dip again.

Max casually sat down beside Cole and asked, "So how are you feeling about me being gay?"

"Do I get to pick my brother-in-law?" Cole asked, not taking his eyes off of his game.

"I'm nowhere close to getting married, silly." Max laughed.

"I better be your best man!" Cole shouted while shooting down an alien on his first person shooter.

"If you can protect me from an alien invasion like that, we have a deal!" Max smiled. He truly had an amazing younger brother.

"I don't think Dad likes it that you're gay," Cole said

bluntly.

"He's going to have to get used to it!" Max said. Thankfully his dad was at work at the moment. His mom was making them chocolate chip cookies in the kitchen.

"You should kiss a guy in front him!" Cole sounded like he had the most genius plan.

"Are you trying to get me kicked out?" Max glared at Cole.

Max grabbed a controller and jumped in to defend earth from the aliens. He was not as good as his brother, but he still enjoyed playing. On occasion, Max would shoot his brother, just to mess with him. It surprised Max how much Cole got into his video games. If only he could make a viable career out of it.

"You're pretty good for a fa- I mean a gay guy!" Cole shouted.

"Yeah, you better watch your mouth! You'll get grounded again!" Max warned.

Just then, Max's mom walked in with a plate of hot chocolate chip cookies. The cookies were perfectly gooey, just like the boys liked them. Max's mom sat down and started asking Cole questions about his game. Max figured she did this to give him a break from Cole's crazy ideas. Otherwise, she would never have an interest in video games.

Once Cole got engrossed in his game again, Max's mom turned to him and suggested, "We should keep Cole quiet about the whole gay thing around your father. He needs some time to adjust without it being talked about all the time."

"If I was straight, we would be able to talk about it constantly!" Max argued.

"I understand, trust me. One of my friends from high school was gay, and he wanted to be treated like anyone else, just like I'm sure you do too. Your dad doesn't see things that way." His mom tried to comfort him the best she could.

The overall mood of the room plummeted when Max's dad arrived back home. Everyone stayed rather quiet, only talking about superficial things. Nobody was willing to dig deep and face the elephant in the room. Max's dad acted as if Max had never come out in the first place. His dad's raw attitude really pissed Max off.

To avoid the emotional quicksand that was his father, Max went upstairs to practice his saxophone. He began playing *Somewhere Over The Rainbow*. To him, the song meant that life would be brighter after coming out. Despite his dad, he still believed it would be. Things would go from black and white to beautiful colors. Too bad his dad was color-blind.

He closed his eyes and began playing the melody. He got so into it, he could have sworn he heard a voice singing the words. When he opened his eyes, he realized there was someone singing. His mom stood there singing every word as he played. Her voice was really remarkable. Max was ready to take her on tour.

"I just wanted to make sure you're ok," she said after the song ended.

"Can a tornado just come through and take me away to Oz?" Max asked longingly.

"Well, you won't be able to fit Cooper in a basket! Plus, you'd run into your father. I'm pretty sure he doesn't have a brain!" Max's mom joked and lightened the mood.

"Things just feel so tense in this house. I didn't want anything to change when I came out!" Max said with a sigh.

"Give it time. I'm sure you weren't comfortable with being gay after just one day. It'll take your father even longer." She rubbed her fingers through Max's hair.

Max thought for a minute, then said, "I just thought there was no place like home."

Chapter 4

Two years before coming out...

Max and Cole sat in the back pew at church playing a
game of tic-tac-toe on the back of the church program. Max
was sure to let Cole win a couple of times to be fair to the
little guy. They rarely paid any attention in church. Max
considered himself a Christian and wanted to follow the
Bible. He always got bored during service. His dad would try
to urge he and his brother to listen. He would tell them the
most important service could come at any time.

For some reason, his mom didn't show much interest in
church, or in Christianity in general. Max always wondered
why that was, but his family wasn't very open with each
other. Somehow, despite their extreme differences, Max's
parents made it work. They rarely argued and always showed
each other affection. They respected one another's
differences. Max admired them for that.

As Max began to draw the winning X on the paper, he
heard the preacher say, "Now we all know that marriage is

between a committed man and woman, but how are we to treat those who believe otherwise?" The preacher continued talking about loving the sinner and hating the sin. He stressed the importance of sharing the Gospel and the truth with those who have turned their backs on God.

Max's muscles began to tighten. His breathing got heavy, and his face turned red. He had been wrestling with his attractions for such a long time, and it made him exhausted. He glanced over to make sure his parents didn't see the tears that were forming in his eyes. When he saw he was in the clear, he ran out the back doors and went into the restroom.

His breathing got even heavier as he slid down the wall and onto the floor. His emotions were too strong for him to care that he was on dirty tiles. He began sobbing as he thought about the preacher's words. *Love the sinner, hate the sin!* kept playing in his head. This sin was such a huge part of his life, and he hated it every single day.

He pressed his hand against his heart, praying it would stop beating so fast. How was he supposed to keep all of this a secret if he freaked out every time he heard someone talk about homosexuality? As soon as the words hit his ears, it was like a switch flipped in his brain.

He finally stepped out of the restroom after giving himself some time to calm down. Everyone was standing up and gathering in the lobby saying their goodbyes at the end of the service. *Thank God it's over!* Max went and joined his family. His mom gave him a concerned look. Max just smiled and looked away. He couldn't let his pain show.

They always went to eat at this little Chinese buffet after

services. Cole never ceased to play with the crab legs, pretending they were his fingers. He didn't actually like crab legs, so Max would devour them for his brother. Cole only ate their chicken tenders. Max believed they were made from cat meat.

"It's not cat!" Cole argued, speaking far too loudly.

"Don't yell so loud, Cole!" His mom glared at Max for bringing up the meat issue.

"My bad, just didn't want him to start meowing involuntarily from all of the cat!" Max laughed.

"Maybe you'll drown because crabs are from the ocean!" Cole used his best comeback.

Before leaving, they all got fortune cookies. The Stevensons went around and read their fortunes. That day was full of repeat fortunes and stupid facts. Max wasn't sure what his fortune even meant. It read, "Fight yourself, and you'll always lose."

As they were driving home in the family minivan, his dad began talking about the service. Max knew this was bound to happen, but it didn't stop him from praying it wouldn't. He tried to ignore it and let his parents do all of the talking. He could always count on his mother to have plenty to say about that day's church sermon.

"I have a problem with a lot of what Pastor Mike said today," Max's mom confessed. "Why should we be so concerned with other people's sin? Isn't that judging? We need to worry about ourselves! Plus, I see being gay as a part of who someone is. It's not a decision that gay people choose!"

Max breathed a little easier after hearing his mother say that. Would his mom be ok with her own son being gay? Max was still trying to fight the attractions, but maybe he didn't have to. Maybe his mom was right.

"I'm sorry, honey, but it is a sin. It clearly states it in the Bible. It's unnatural," Max's dad replied. "Nobody is born that way."

This went on for a while. Max decided to put on his headphones. He played his music softly, just in case his parents said something he needed to hear. Cole was asleep to the left of him. He wondered what his thoughts would be on the whole situation. Would he even know what the word gay meant?

His mom peered in the rearview mirror to see Cole sleeping and Max listening to music. She looked at her husband and said, "What would you do if one of our boys were gay?" She stared at him, eagerly awaiting his answer.

Max's eyes also peered at his father. He could hear every single word, and he knew he wanted to know the words that would follow. He clenched his fists and awaited his father's answer. His dad seemed to be thinking really hard. The suspense was torturing Max even more.

"Honestly, I'd be embarrassed to have a gay son." The words finally came out of his dad's mouth.

"I've known many gay and lesbian people in my life. Nothing about them seems wrong at all!" his mom argued back.

"They may be nice people, but it's not normal!" His dad stopped at a red light.

Max felt like he had just been stabbed in the heart. There was no way he could accept being gay. He wanted to make his father proud of him. He wanted to be a good Christian boy so that maybe he could be closer to his father. Now, he knew what he had to do to achieve that goal. He unclenched his fists and saw blood in the palms of his hands where his nails had dug into them.

Max avoided his parents once they arrived home from church. He assumed that they knew something was wrong, and if they started questioning him, things could get tense. Cole wanted to play games with him, but his mind was far too heavy to focus on a game. Max let his fear isolate him all day.

Searching for something to make him happy, Max wandered into the world of Internet porn. He was happy for the instant gratification. It made him forget about his worries. However, he realized that what gratified him in that moment added to the issue at hand. Even trying to escape his problem made him run right back into it.

That night, Max decided he would make a promise to God. He vowed to never be gay. He refused to choose that lifestyle if it meant going against God and his father. He promised he would continue to hate his sin. If he never loved that part of himself, eventually it was bound to go away. So, he would look at that side of himself with disgust and anger.

To lighten up his mood, he decided to take Cooper for a walk. His black and white husky always loved walking around the neighborhood and seeing the other dogs. Max loved making Cooper happy. He got Cooper for his fourteenth birthday, and it had always been the best present he had ever been blessed with. To Max, there was nothing like the unconditional love of his dog.

As Max and Cooper turned a corner, Max saw a shirtless jogger on the other side of the road. The sweat glistening from the runner's body enthralled Max. He hadn't realized he was staring until Cooper began to bark at the guy. Max was caught off guard when the guy stopped running and smiled at him. Max waved sheepishly then headed back to the house.

His mind raced all night. He was so mad that he felt a strong attraction to the jogging guy in his neighborhood. Hours flew by and his thoughts kept him restless. No matter how tired he got, sleep just wouldn't welcome him. He couldn't hold back his tears any longer. They began to pour onto his pillow. He cried for the next hour before he finally fell asleep, released from the day's pain and confusion.

Chapter 5

Max stared at himself in the bathroom mirror and gave himself a pep talk to start the day. It was the first day back at school after his week and a half fall break. It was also his first day at school after telling his parents about his sexuality. It was time to let his peers in on his long-kept secret. He was positive they would all take it well. After all, he was still the same Max. He styled up his straight blond hair and headed out the door.

He smiled during his fifteen-minute drive to Sandersville High. He was anxious to see what his friends would have to say. Even better, he wouldn't have to hide anymore. There was such a sweet relief in that thought. Hell, Max hadn't even begun to think about finding himself a cute boyfriend. Surely there were more boys that were out other than the ever so flaming Nick.

Nick had helped Max come to terms with himself. They rarely talked anymore after things got tense and awkward between them. Every time he saw Nick, Max's face became flushed from the memories of their last night hanging out. It was a very eye opening time for Max, but that was another story. Today was about focusing on his close friends!

Max had a tight-knit group of friends that consisted of three people. Adrianna and Jess were the females of the group. They were both on the cheerleading team and were the typical popular girls. They didn't use their powers for evil though. They were actually very nice. Jess had gorgeous blonde hair and green eyes. She was very smart and was working towards becoming a nurse. Adrianna's fiery red hair matched her intense personality. She always made sure she got what she wanted, no matter how much attitude she had to use.

His best friend was Tyler. He and Tyler were in band class together. Max played the saxophone while Tyler jammed out on percussion. They had been friends since freshman year. Originally, Max wanted to play percussion so he asked Tyler to teach him. That never worked out, but he got a great friend out of trying.

They all had lunch together after third period. Max figured that would be the best time to tell them. He had plenty of time for his brain to fill up with worrisome thoughts as he ran around the track during his third period gym class. He ran a much slower two miles because of all the mental distractions going on. Would he have the guts to say the words he needed to say once again?

After gym class, all the boys got in the showers and cleaned up for lunch. Self-control was hard for Max when it came to shower time. He forced himself to not stare at the other guys, especially Tyler. Tyler had beautiful dark curls and a great slim body. Although Max crushed on him, he knew they would always only be friends.

"Little slow out there today!" Tyler said while turning on the shower head next to Max. The hot steamy water hit his face and slid down his body.

"A lot on my mind." Max stared straight ahead. He'd never looked at Tyler naked, and he didn't plan to now.

Max told him he would talk about it at lunch as they dried off and got dressed. Max was actually getting quite eager to talk to his friends about boys and what life was like in the closet. He hoped and prayed his being gay wouldn't change the vibe in the showers. Surely everyone noticed that he didn't stare anyone down. Any time he would see one of his classmate's naked body, it was mostly by accident.

It was pizza Thursday at lunch so the whole table was in a pretty good mood. The school had a local pizza joint called A Pizza Paradise that delivered to them. No more of that crappy rectangle pizza imposter for them. Max was thankful for the smiles that would start his conversation off right.

"Hey guys, I want to tell you all something," Max said with a lump in his throat.

"OMG me too! Thanks for reminding me!" Adrianna replied while pushing back her red hair from her face. "You first!"

Max told her to go ahead so he could have more time before the truth was dropped. Adrianna went on about how she was pretty sure the new kid, Joseph, was into her. Max hadn't even noticed a new kid around the school. He was too preoccupied with his own shit to even care about new school members. Nevertheless, he took interest in her story because he really cared about his friends. They were his life outside of his family.

"So, what were you gonna say, Max?" Jess spoke up. She seemed rushed to end Adrianna's news.

"I um... Well you all know I've had some off days lately?" he started as everyone nodded. "Well, I was fighting with something, but I'm not fighting it anymore. I just wanted to tell you all that I'm gay."

Once again Max had to survive some silence as the news absorbed into their brains. Adrianna and Jess spoke up with support and love. Jess said she had suspected, and Adrianna said she was ready for guy talk and girls' nights. Max laughed and let out a smile as he glanced over at Tyler. Tyler was staring at him with his brow furrowed. Without a word he stood up from the table and walked away.

The table got silent as the symptoms of anxiety crept back into Max's body like an old friend. Sweat began forming on his forehead. His heart sped up and his breath got short. He glanced at the girls for support, but they didn't know what to say. He gulped as he asked himself, "Did I just lose my best friend?"

A dark cloud followed Max during the rest of the school day. Tyler ignored him during their band class, the final class of the day. Max had to fight to keep the tears from pouring out during his ride home. He had thought that Tyler would still be his friend after he came out. What went wrong? No matter how hard he tried to understand why Tyler was so upset, he couldn't think of a single reason.

Max brought his dinner into his bedroom that night to avoid talking to his family. He had to be alone to deal with the tough emotions he was feeling. Otherwise, he would have to push them away which only hurt his family more. There was a sense of comfort in being alone that Max needed more than anything in that moment.

Max was comforted that night by music and tears. He sent about twenty text messages, all of which were ignored. To avoid breaking something valuable, Max punched his pillow, then he slammed his face into the pillow to scream. Violent sobs shook Max's body. He had never felt more alone in his entire life.

Max got very little sleep that night. The unwelcome negative thoughts poured in. He couldn't stop them. Did Tyler think he was a freak? Should he have kept it all a secret? Would Tyler tell the whole school before he was ready? He closed his eyes as he imagined a noose. He pictured sliding his head into the noose while standing on a wobbly chair. The chair slipped out from under him, and he saw himself dangling there, problem free. Peace flooded his soul as he finally began to slip into a peaceful sleep. Why was suicide the only thought that could relax him?

Chapter 6

Twenty-two months before coming out...

Just like that, the body was hanging over the unguessed phrase. Max had just destroyed Cole in a game of hang-man. Of course, he never expected his younger brother to guess "John 3:16." Max was on a huge Bible kick lately. He was relying on that good old book to save him from his impure thoughts. He just had to dedicate enough time to God, and then he would be cured.

After church that day, Max got dropped off at Tyler's house to work on some homework. He and Tyler knew if they didn't study for the math test they had the following day, they would be screwed. They tried their hardest to focus on the problems in their math books, but they lacked the motivation to study very long. That's when Tyler got an idea.

"Dude, want to check out my porn magazine?" Tyler had a mischievous grin on his face.

Max's face turned red at the suggestion. They had joked about sex before, but they had never looked at porn together.

Out of fear of Tyler thinking he was gay, he decided to go along with it. Maybe it would help Max with the unwanted feelings he had. Surely seeing naked women would kick his mind into straight mode.

Tyler reached under his bed and pulled out the magazine. He started flipping through the pages and ogling at all the boobs he found. "Wow, look at those knockers! I'd kill to get my hands on them!" Tyler said with a smile on his face. He looked at Max waiting on his opinion of the naked woman.

"Hell yeah man! The things I would do to her!" Max tried to make himself believe the words he was saying.

Max's heart started pounding when he noticed a hint of excitement coming from Tyler's pants. No matter how bad he wanted to, he couldn't glance away. Before he knew it, his own excitement began to show. His face became flushed as he shoved his hands in his pockets to hide his boner.

Tyler turned to a page that revealed a girl and a guy going at it. Max was engulfed in guilt because he couldn't look away from the guy. He was a bit too hairy for Max's taste, but he had the right body. If asked, Max could describe the male porn star perfectly, but he knew nothing about the girl's appearance.

"Maybe we should stop," Max suggested. "I'm really trying to get close to God, and this isn't helping."

Tyler rolled his eyes and put the magazine away. "If I didn't know any better, I'd think you were gay. Who wants to quit looking at porn?" he said, teasingly.

Max laughed it off, but on the inside he was cursing himself. Why couldn't he be more like Tyler? He just wanted to feel normal for once! He knew he could never tell Tyler about his inappropriate thoughts. He would go to the grave with this secret. But if he didn't tell somebody, he would go insane!

That evening when Max got home he went into his room and opened his laptop. He went to Google and looked up some Christian counselors that helped guys struggling with same-sex attraction. He pulled out his phone and dialed the first number he saw. He paced the room waiting for someone to pick up the phone.

"Pure Hope Counseling, this is Monica. How may I help you?" a friendly voice spoke.

Max informed the kind lady about what was going on. She told him all about their program. They had group counseling along with solo sessions. They had plenty of members which made Max feel more at ease. He wasn't alone. Everything was sounding perfect until Monica asked a question that derailed Max's plan.

"How will you be paying for your sessions?" she asked.

"Oh, I hadn't thought of that. I can't ask my parents, they don't know," Max said, sighing.

Max found out he needed his parents' permission to even be in the program. Frustrated, he hung up the phone and threw his body on the bed. He began praying for an answer to his dilemma. He had to do something. He felt so alone in his head. A few tears began to trickle down his face.

For the first time, he thought about how much easier things would be if he wasn't alive. He wouldn't be battling the confusion in his head. He wouldn't have to be a disappointment to his friends and family. There would be no more fighting the wrong feelings he was bombarded with on a daily basis. He would be free. Unfortunately, he was pretty sure people who killed themselves went to Hell. Suicide was a sin.

Suddenly, Max had an idea. He had yet to go to his church's youth group held on Wednesday's. That could be his answered prayer. He could go and talk to the youth pastor about his problems and finally get some help. His dad had been pushing him to attend anyway. He sighed with relief and prayed for Wednesday to come faster. He had to get help. He had to become normal.

In the meantime, Max started to focus on changing certain mannerisms. He would stop saying "like" all of the time. Also, he really needed to stop putting his hand on his hip. That was way too effeminate for him to continue doing. He got his journal out and made a list of everything he needed to stop doing.

With everything he wrote, his self-hatred grew. He hadn't realized how gay he acted until he put his mannerisms on a list. Why hadn't anyone told him to stop doing these flamboyant things? Surely other people noticed them! Max would make certain nobody would notice ever again.

Max thought about how he needed to stop his addiction to gay porn. He was pretty sure he needed to cease masturbation, too. On the next page of his journal, he drew a cross. He made seven boxes inside the cross. Each day he went without masturbating, he would fill in a box. He was determined to fill the cross to the top.

With all of this planning, Max imagined the gay feelings fleeing from his body. Satan had no idea who he was messing with. In Max's drawer, he had a cross necklace that he hadn't worn in quite some time. He put it on and prayed, "Lord, give me the strength to be a warrior! Let me defeat this struggle!"

Chapter 7

Knock knock knock! Max's eyes rushed open at the sound. He saw his mom creak open the door and look inside. She wore a worried look as she saw him lying there. What time was it? Had he slept through school? He looked at the time on his phone and saw that it was quarter after five. *Shit!*

"I'm so sorry mom! I forgot to set my alarm!" Max said.

"So, you slept until five?" his mom replied. "Are you ok?"

Max lied and said that everything was ok. He could tell his mom wasn't convinced. She didn't push the issue, but she told him he needed to get up and make something of what he had left of the day. Max managed to push himself out of the bed and get into the shower. Overwhelmed with emotion, he sat on the shower floor and cried. Things were supposed to be getting better, but they weren't.

Max finished getting ready like a zombie who hadn't had brains in days. He wasn't even sure why he was getting cleaned up. He had wasted his whole day already. He wanted to go back to bed and start all over again. He didn't even feel like eating dinner. He was too flooded with disappointment in himself.

While Max's mom cooked, his dad lectured him about missing school. Max knew his dad was right about everything, so he decided there was no use in trying to defend himself. Although he didn't say it, Max assumed his dad thought he was a failure. Since Max had come out, he felt a negative tension between him and his dad.

Max let his mood sink even lower thinking what his father's thoughts might be. He guessed that his dad thought he was going to Hell. Max tried to mentally prepare himself for the day his dad tried to save him from his homosexuality. After all, his dad was quite the evangelical Christian, preaching to everyone that bought a car at his work.

After Max managed to eat a few bites of his mom's grilled chicken, he was startled by an alert on his phone. He opened his messages to see a new one from Jess. She and Adrianna were having a sleep over, and they invited Max to join. After getting permission from his mom, he packed some clothes and headed out of the house. He already felt better, knowing he wouldn't be alone with his thoughts all night again.

He heard his father ask his mother before he could get out of the door, "You're letting him stay overnight with girls?"

"He's gay. I don't think we have to worry about him getting one of them pregnant," his mom responded with a laugh. "Plus, he's had a rough day!"

"Well, with any luck, the night will straighten him out!"

his dad said in a voice that meant he wasn't joking.

Max rolled his eyes and rushed out the door. His mind kept dwelling on his father's comment about the girls turning him straight. Why did his dad have to be so inconsiderate? Frustrated, Max punched his steering wheel. The rest of the way to Jess's house, he took deep breaths so he wouldn't be on edge all night.

While Max and the girls were watching *The Notebook*, Adrianna asked why he wasn't at school. He informed her about his miserable night and his hurt over how Tyler had reacted. He even added on his previous struggle with depression and how he thought it would all be over after coming out. It felt so good to let it all out.

"Oh honey, Tyler just needs time. He's a boy. That's how they are," Adrianna responded.

Max got irritated at her response. "I'm a boy too, you know. Just because I'm gay doesn't make me less of a boy. Please don't treat me differently."

Adrianna apologized and decided to change the subject. "So, Joseph and I are supposed to hang out tomorrow! He totally has a thing for me. He better make a move, or else I'll have to!"

Max got jealous at the thought of Adrianna dating. He had finally come out, and he wanted to meet someone so badly. After all of his suffering, he deserved it, right? Only, he had no clue where to even start. Perhaps he should ask the girls for some dating advice. "So, um... how should I go about meeting somebody?"

Jess's face lit up as she said, "Yes! We must get you a

boyfriend! Have you tried using dating apps?"

Max admitted that he had been on some in the past, but they all seemed sketchy! All of the guys either wanted him for his dick or his ass, which he had never shown most of them. There was the one incident which he tried his hardest to push out of his mind. He was still embarrassed over what he had done before coming out.

He shook that thought out of his mind and said, "There has to be another way to meet gay guys!"

Adrianna suggested that he start wearing rainbow clothing every day. Jess suggested he should wait and let it happen naturally. He didn't like either of those options. If only Tyler could have been gay. They could live happily ever after! Max cringed at the thought of Tyler as the hurt returned to his heavy heart.

Adrianna saw the mood shift in Max and decided to ask him and Jess if they wanted to join her on her date the following day. They both had no plans for Saturday so they agreed to go. Hopefully, it would lift Max's mood. They spent the rest of the night discussing what they would do. That evening, Max was blessed with a full night's sleep.

The next day, they pulled up to the Mall and shuffled into the food court. They grabbed a table and waited on Joseph to arrive. Thankfully, Joseph was totally cool with a group hang out. He needed more friends anyway, considering he had just moved seven hours away from his old home in Richmond, Virginia. Perhaps this could be a group that all of the members could benefit from.

"This guy isn't homophobic, is he?" Max asked, wearing

worry all over his face.

"Well, I never thought to ask, but he doesn't seem like he is to me. I'm sure it'll be fine. If he hates gays, I'll stop talking to him!" Adrianna said, comforting Max.

The fact that Adrianna was willing to give up a boy for Max's comfort was the sweetest thing she had ever proposed. What possibly could have went wrong in Tyler's mind that he was not able to react like Adrianna and Jess? Perhaps, in time, the girls would talk some sense into him.

"There he is!" Adrianna nearly shrieked as she pointed toward the mall entrance.

Max stared with his mouth wide open. Joseph was absolutely stunning. His sandy blond hair was pushed up into a little swoop above his beautiful clear face. His tight black dress shirt hugged his slim body perfectly. Max's favorite parts were Joseph's award-winning smile and his beautiful blue eyes.

Max had to force himself to snap out of it when Joseph made it to the table. *Shit, I'm crushing on a straight guy,* he thought.

Adrianna introduced Joseph to the group. They decided to stroll around the mall. Adrianna and Joseph walked shoulder to shoulder the whole time. It was clear they were kicking it off well. Max and Jess had their own conversation, with the occasional group interaction. It wasn't the perfect group dynamic yet, and that sort of upset Max. He wanted to get to know the cool new kid more, but Adrianna had a monopoly on him.

"So, Joseph, what do you like to do for fun?" Max asked.

He had to make the group feel like one.

"I'm a writer. I enjoy writing poetry!" he responded proudly.

"Oh my gosh! That is so adorable!" Adrianna perked up. Jess rolled her eyes.

"That really is awesome! Maybe we can hang out sometime," Max added. He needed to replace Tyler. He lacked the close connection to a boy like he once had. It left a hole in his heart.

Joseph agreed as Adrianna glared at Max. Max felt slightly guilty, but he was just trying to make a new friend. It's not like he could turn Joseph gay.

After they spent the day together, it was time for everyone to go home. They said their goodbyes, and Adrianna gave Joseph a peck on the cheek. Jealousy surged through Max. He went home with his shoulders slumped. He wasn't sure if the day helped him as much as he needed it to.

While he got comfortable in bed that night, he pulled out his iPhone and opened up the App Store. Frustrated, he looked up Grindr. It was the gay dating/hookup app that was known for its slutty guys who just wanted sex. It seemed like the only way he could try to find a love of his own, only finding love on that app was like trying to find a needle in a haystack or a heart in a stack of dick pics!

Chapter 8

Twenty-two months before coming out...

Max's dad was rushing Max to the church. His dad needed to be at the car dealership ten minutes ago. Max felt a little uncomfortable going ninety miles an hour on the interstate, but he trusted that his dad knew enough about cars to not wreck one. Still, if he went much faster, Max would be meeting Jesus, not the youth leader.

"I wish I could go in with you and meet the leader. I never got the chance to introduce myself," his dad said disappointedly.

"That would be like walking me into class, dad. I'm seventeen. That would be weird." Max rolled his eyes, glad his dad had to work.

Max walked into the Youth Group meeting fifteen minutes early. He was hoping to get a quick word in with the youth pastor before it started. He looked around the empty room and saw no one. He took a seat and waited for somebody to arrive. The longer he waited, the more unsure he was about revealing his secret to the youth pastor.

"You're here early! I'm Ryan, the youth leader. What's your name?" a voice said from in front of Max. Ryan looked to be in his early thirties with a few gray hairs peeking out of the brown. He wore a brown vest that Max adored, and he had a positive energy with the words he spoke.

Max looked up and introduced himself to Ryan. Ryan asked him if he would like to help set up the stage for service. Max was glad that Ryan seemed friendly. While he was plugging in a microphone, Max spoke up and said, "I was wondering if I could talk to you about something important after service?"

"Of course! I'd be glad to! Always eager to meet new members," Ryan replied with a smile on his face.

Kids gradually started filling up the room and taking seats. Max didn't know anyone, so he sat on his own and stressed over the conversation that he and Ryan would soon be having.

He only picked up on a couple of points during the service. It was about loving yourself as much as God loves you. He wasn't sure how much God could love him with the sinful desires that he couldn't let go of.

Please, God, let this conversation go well, he prayed to himself during the closing prayer. *I'm trying to follow your will and make my family proud. I don't want to be a freak. I don't want to like other guys. It's not fair, God. I just want to be normal. Please.*

As everyone shuffled out of the building, Max paced the room nervously. How was he going to explain what was going on? He had never told anyone about his feelings. Would he be shunned from the youth group? He was second guessing his decision when Ryan walked up and told him to have a seat. He took a deep breath and sat down with him.

"So tell me a little about yourself, Max," Ryan said.

Max went on to tell him about his family and his interests. He told Ryan about how much he loved band class. He also explained to him about his best friend, Tyler. Max admitted he had no idea what he wanted to do after high school was over. He went on and on, unable to bring up the reason he came in the first place.

"Sounds like you have a pretty blessed life, my man!" Ryan said. "What were you wanting to talk about?"

There was no more avoiding it. It was time to talk about the hard stuff. Max took a deep breath and said, "Well, I need help. I have this problem. I haven't told anyone else about this yet. I'm not attracted to girls. I'm attracted to guys, though. I know it's wrong, and I know I'm going to go to Hell if I'm gay, and I don't know what to do!"

Suddenly, Max felt a sense of calm. He had finally let out the truth, and he felt so much better. It was like a weight had been lifted off his shoulders. He was no longer carrying the burden alone. He looked at Ryan, ready to find the answers to his problems. He was ready to become a changed man.

"That's tough, Max, but it's not uncommon. Many Christians struggle with being attracted to the same sex. What you need to know is this: God didn't make you gay. There is hope!" Ryan said. "I'm not saying it will be easy, but you don't have to suffer forever."

"But how do I make it stop? I've prayed for quite some time about this. When Pastor Mike talked about it, I knew I had to do something. I just feel so gross!" Max added.

Ryan went on talking about the power of prayer. He informed Max that consistency was key. He had to keep powering through his prayers and refusing to give in to the devil's plan. He talked about the beauty of Heaven and how important it was to not give that up. He gave Max the faith he needed to go on fighting this sin that plagued his life.

Ryan prayed with Max and asked him if he would be interested in weekly meetings. Max was thrilled that Ryan was willing to take an interest. He felt that this was exactly what he needed. He quickly accepted the offer to meet up and fight this struggle together. Max said goodbye to Ryan and left with a renewed sense of confidence. Nothing could stand in his way now!

After his dad picked him up from the church, Max told him about how much he enjoyed going. He raved about the music and how nice Ryan was. The only thing he was unsure about was the other kids. He wasn't sure he would fit in with anyone. His dad told him he just needed to give it some time.

"You know, I'm really proud of you!" Max's dad said. "I was really praying you would try it out. After your grandfather died, I turned to the church. Church was the one place your grandfather loved more than anything, so I wanted to feel close to him. I needed to feel like he was still here. Words can't describe how much Christ has healed my hurt."

Max's grandfather died when Max was only five. He

knew it had affected his father, but he hadn't been sure how much. His dad had never talked about it before now. Suddenly Max realized how being a Christian could bring him closer to his father. So, not only would he fight to become straight, but he would also have a better relationship with his dad.

When he got home, he quickly pulled out his phone and rang Tyler. He expressed his excitement about youth group. When Tyler showed even the least bit of interest, Max invited him to join the next week. Max smiled from ear to ear when Tyler accepted the invitation. Now, Max wouldn't feel so alone there. Also, he could hide his disinterest in naked women by claiming it wasn't Christ-like.

For the first night in a while, Max fell asleep with a smile on his face. *Never Let Go,* his favorite Christian song, played in the background as he slowly drifted off, thanking God for the day that he had. He prayed about his sexuality, and he also prayed for his father. He asked God to take care of his grandfather and told Him to pass along a hello for Max.

That night, he dreamed about his wedding day. He was standing at the end of the aisle as the wedding march began to play. He smiled as he watched his bride walk down the aisle to stand in front of him. They said their vows and got ready for the kiss. As Max lifted the veil, he was shocked to see the face of a man.

Chapter 9

As time passed, Tyler refused to speak to Max. He couldn't understand how someone who was there for him for so long could just drop him like a fly. Surely he had more worth than an annoying insect! He began to question their entire friendship. He played their relationship back through his mind, trying to find out where he went wrong. Could it really be that Tyler was just a homophobe?

To fill his time when he wasn't hanging out with Jess, Adrianna, and Joseph, he scrolled through Grindr to find some dates. When he finally found someone who wasn't just looking for sex, he would invite him out for coffee. Throughout this time, he began to see how hard dating really was. How long would it take for him to find someone compatible with who he was?

His first date was beyond awkward. He met up with a tall, lanky science nerd at the local coffee shop. They had some really good chats online so Max expected nothing less than a good time. Only, Mr. Lanky decided he didn't want to speak much in person. No matter how hard Max tried to start a conversation, it quickly died. It got to the point where Max began talking about random pictures hanging on the walls. When he left, Mr. Lanky said he wanted to talk again. *Again?! You didn't even talk!* Max thought.

Then, there was the guy who only talked about himself. Sure, Max found him super attractive, but he didn't feel very special around him. Not once did he ask Max about his life. If Max was into hookups, this would be the perfect candidate because there was no way in hell a long term relationship could happen with this hot narcissistic ass. The guy said he would talk to him soon, but Max never heard back from him.

To cure his loneliness, Max spent his nights watching porn. He enjoyed the hot doctor scenarios. Something about the element of surprise in these sexual adventures thrilled Max. Slowly, his pain would go away as he spent time with his hand and Dr. Dick. It was only a temporary fix though, and he knew that. He would only feel lonelier after the deed was done. There was no cuddling his laptop, no matter how warm it had gotten. He needed human touch.

Eventually, Adrianna and Joseph became a couple. As much as Max enjoyed hanging out with his friend group, he was covered in jealousy when he saw them kiss. He and Jess would make gagging noises and tease them the whole time. At least he wasn't a total third wheel. He wouldn't know what to do without his fourth wheel. He needed Jess to keep him sane.

Because the town of Sandersville had no real source of entertainment, they all got together once again at the mall. It was as if they expected new things to go on sale every day.

Of course, it took Jess three times to see something she liked before she would buy it. She liked to be safe with her money, unlike Adrianna.

"I promise we will find someone for you!" Jess said with more confidence than Max had.

"What if none of the guys in this town are a match for me? I'm going to grow to be a cat person," he replied with a disgusted voice.

"Hey! I like cats!" She pulled her phone out and showed him a picture of an adorable kitten.

"Pussy just isn't my thing," he responded with a smirk. They shared a good laugh over that one.

After the mall, they went to a nearby restaurant to get some buffalo wings. When the waiter popped up to get their drink orders, Max had to hide his shock over how attractive this guy was. His name tag revealed that his name was Scott, and he was gorgeous. He had deep green eyes and dark brown hair with the perfect amount of scruff on his face. Max could barely get out his drink order.

"Somebody is crushing!" Joseph pointed out.

"Is it that obvious?" Max blushed.

The entire time they were there, Scott made eye contact with Jess. Max knew this meant he was straight. This didn't stop him from getting bold and leaving his phone number on the receipt. Everyone was shocked at his bravery. Max didn't consider it to be brave. He considered it to be desperate.

The next morning, after there was no call from Scott, Max woke up to a friend request on Facebook. He couldn't believe his eyes when he saw it was from Scott himself. As it turns out, Scott couldn't read his number, so he got his name from the credit card receipt. Max's heart began jumping for joy. Scott actually was gay, and he wanted to contact Max! Pure excitement overflowed Max.

Despite invitation after invitation to hang out, Scott kept declining. He used excuse after excuse. Finally Max grew tired of trying. "What is your deal? Are we ever going to hang out?" Max texted.

"Listen, my ex is constantly around, and he wants to work things out. I haven't fully let him go," Scott responded, spilling the truth.

So even though Scott was still confused about his own relationship problems, he still dragged Max into his world by sending the friend request. Max didn't know why Scott would go through all of that effort for nothing. He began to wish he never had gone to get wings that day.

He returned to the world of Grindr and began talking to guys again. Occasionally, he would give in and send naughty images to the horny recipients. Although he felt guilty, it was a huge ego boost to him. This went on for weeks until he stumbled upon a new account. A cute college kid named Lee was standing with his friend at a basketball game in the profile picture. He didn't look gay at all. He was buff with a very sharp looking brown buzz cut. His broad shoulders made Max want to put his hands on him right at that moment. To top it off, he had the jawline of a god! Max quickly sent a message to his own personal Hercules.

When Lee responded to Max's message, Max felt a thrill run through his veins. All it took was a simple hello, and

Max allowed himself to obsess over this hunk. As they talked, Max tried to keep himself from getting too enveloped in this stranger.

Their conversation continued for days. They talked about their love of music. Lee enjoyed going to concerts and mentioned taking Max to one someday. Max allowed his mind to get carried away as he imagined a future with this cute stranger. Perhaps he wouldn't have to search much longer.

When the idea of hanging out in person got brought up, a disturbing truth came out. Lee had a boyfriend who lived in a city an hour away. Yet, he still wanted to hang out with Max. Against his better judgment, Max's desire to meet Lee in person wouldn't go away. They would just have to be friends; no matter how attractive Lee was.

Max knew relationships didn't always last forever. How many breakup movies had he seen? Adults were getting divorced every day. There was still a chance that he and Lee could be together one day. He decided to remain hopeful. They hadn't even met, but Max still felt a strong connection. He could only imagine what it would be like to meet him. He wouldn't have to imagine for long, because Lee had invited him to a cookout his friends were having. Max took a deep breath as he hit the send button on his message agreeing to go to the cookout.

Not long after they talked, he spilled the beans to Jess. She was shocked that Max would agree to meet a guy who was taken. She went on and on about how she didn't want him getting hurt, but Max was stubborn. He refused to change his mind. He craved the connection with another guy. He didn't care about the cost. Also, he wasn't convinced this was going to have a bad ending. It could be the start of something beautiful.

One thing Max had to do before meeting Lee was to stalk his Facebook page. He scrolled through years of pictures, admiring Lee's beauty. Panic struck Max as he accidentally liked one of his pictures from three years ago. He quickly took off the like and hoped that Lee wouldn't notice it was ever there.

Lee's life looked so perfect from a social media standpoint. He had tons of friends and went to numerous events. Max was filled with envy from looking through Lee's many adventures. Lee seemed to have a blast at Coachella a few years back. Also, his Hawaii vacation pictures amazed Max. He admired Lee even more when he discovered that Lee was planning to be a news anchor. Max knew good and well that it took charisma to handle a job like that.

Before Max shut his eyes to drift off into dreamland, a question entered his mind. Did he want to be with Lee, or did he want to be Lee? Perhaps Lee's awesomeness would rub off on Max, and he would be admired as much as he admired Lee? He struggled to fall asleep because of the many scenarios racing through his mind about Lee. Like the kids' saying goes, first comes love, then comes marriage, then comes Max with a baby carriage.

Chapter 10

Twenty-one months before coming out...

Tyler, like Max's mom, wasn't very big on the religious scene. Max wasn't sure how he would handle all of it. Would he make fun of Max for his faith? Ideally, Tyler would pick up on the hope that Max found and would start his own faith journey. Max thought about how special he would feel if Tyler became a Christian because of him. Also, his dad would be so proud of him.

"So just tell me. What am I getting myself into, bro?" Tyler asked cautiously as he waited on his McDonald's order to be ready.

"I don't know. I mean they just sing and have a service and stuff." Max shrugged.

As they chowed down on their food, they talked about how Tyler had never been to church because his parents were atheists. Tyler admitted that he believed there had to be a higher power, but he wasn't sure if it was the Christian God, or something else. He had been meaning to check out some religions but never had the chance.

"You know," Tyler started as he bit into his Big Mac. "My parents laughed at me when I told them where I was going."

"Oh my gosh! Dude, I'm so sorry. You should have the right to find your own answers," Max responded, a little shocked.

"They're very closed-minded about religion, so I expected it," Tyler said, shrugging.

The McDonald's that Max's father dropped them off at was right beside the church. They finished up and walked over for youth group. Max introduced Tyler to Ryan, and they hit it off pretty fast. Ryan was thrilled that he chose to check things out, despite his parents being critical. "The best things can happen when you branch out and take a risk!" Ryan told him.

Max was glad he had taken the risk to fight the homosexual demon inside of him. Now, it was time to pray that Tyler would be glad he came. Throughout all of the service, Max was hoping God was speaking to Tyler. But then, Max was sure God had spoken to him. Ryan's next words struck a chord with Max.

"Just because people grow up in a Christian home or go to church, it doesn't mean they are a Christian. Becoming a Christian requires the magical moment you lay your life down for the Lord. If you want the happiness and joy that I talked about today, you must surrender to God!" Ryan preached with a powerful confidence.

Max had never had that moment of surrender with God.

He had only chosen to believe in Him and fight against his sexual immorality. Max felt a yearning for something in that instant. He yearned for the happiness Ryan described. Too often, he felt a sense of sorrow and self-hatred. He wanted what God had to offer so he could wake up in the morning with a smile.

Ryan informed the youth that they could come forward and accept God into their hearts as the next song played. *Lead Me to The Cross* began to play as a single tear fell down Max's face. This could be his time of hope. He didn't waste another note before walking to the front, kneeling beside a wooden cross, and praying to God.

God, I want the joy that Ryan spoke about today. I want you to live in my heart, make me clean, and get rid of the sadness I feel inside. I know the sadness comes from my impure thoughts about boys so I need help with that. Ryan kneeled beside Max and bowed his head with him as Max continued his silent prayer. *So, in this moment, I ask you to enter my heart and make me yours! Amen!*

Max felt such a relief in that moment. He hadn't even realized that his one tear had become many. As Ryan gave his shoulder a squeeze of congratulations, Max looked over and saw Tyler sobbing at the cross like Max had been. Max quickly walked over and put his hand on Tyler's shoulder as he gave his life to God, too. Max knew this would be the start of something great.

After the service, Max and Tyler sat and talked. Tyler told Max how emotional he got when he heard about the happiness he could have. They went on and on in pure excitement over what had occurred. Tyler got more serious when he brought up how his parents would feel.

"I know they won't understand. I can't tell them. That's too much of a risk!" Tyler said.

Max agreed that he didn't need to tell them right away. He thought that not everything needed to be discussed. After all, he wasn't going to tell Tyler about his attraction to men. Secrets kept people safe, so some things would have to wait for a safer time.

As the weeks went on, Max and Tyler had private Bible studies with Ryan. They all had the best times together while learning about God's love. They laughed, cried, prayed, and drank plenty of coffee. What better place to have a Bible study than a coffee shop? They always left with plenty of energy.

Max gradually thought about naked boys less. He would nevertheless slip up, but he asked for forgiveness every time he would watch two men make love on the Internet. He forced himself to think about Hell, misery, darkness, and a deep depression when he would lust after boys. After all, that's the price he would pay to be gay. He wanted happiness far more than attention from cute boys.

Chapter 11

Max tried pressing the wrinkles from his shirt as he stared into the mirror. *God, I know things have been weird between us lately, but please let this cookout with Lee go well!* Max prayed. *I don't even know if I can pray gay things like that, but I hope You still listen!* He put another glob of gel into his blond hair and tried to keep it all in place. Eventually, he had to deal with how he looked. The cookout was starting soon.

His steering wheel became very sweaty as Max drove to the cookout. There were a couple of moments when he was convinced he should turn around and go back home. Maybe he should listen to Jess and not even meet Lee in person. Yet, every time he almost aborted his plan, he thought of Lee's gorgeous smile.

Max's heart was pounding so rapidly as he walked to the pool deck that he was sure Lee would hear. He saw a bunch of people standing near a grill. He walked in that direction when his eyes finally landed on Lee. He froze in his tracks as Lee looked up and made eye contact. There was no denying the strong chemistry between them, especially when their hands touched for a handshake. There were instant sparks.

"Hi, I'm Max!" *Shit!* "But you knew that already! Sorry!" Max said, giggling nervously.

Lee smiled at Max like he was the cutest thing he had ever seen. "Nice to meet you, cutie," Lee responded with an adorable, crooked smile. Lee had to have known that he was making Max's heart melt like the butter on the rolls at the cookout.

Max was introduced to Lee's friends, and they all sat around a table and enjoyed their food. Max and Lee didn't talk much in the first thirty minutes of the party, but they made some intense eye contact. When Max was offered a beer, he accepted just so that he could impress Lee. Max forced the horse piss colored drink down his throat, hoping it would make it easier to talk to Lee.

It worked. Before he knew it, they were side by side talking like they had known each other for years. They shared coming out stories. Lee laughed about Cole's question regarding what being gay meant. Lee claimed to know all about gay life at that age. He said coming out was easy for him. Max quickly discovered that flirting was, too. When Lee put on his moves, Max reminded himself that Lee was a taken man, yet he didn't want to stop Lee just yet.

After a while, everyone decided they wanted to go swimming. Max didn't bring trunks, but he could always swim in his shorts. Everyone went to one of the girl's apartments and got ready to go to the pool. Max was thrilled when he saw Lee in just his trunks. His heart may have dropped, but his penis did the opposite. He tried his best to pull himself together.

As they walked towards the pool, a cold rain began to pour down, ruining their plans. A few people said they still wanted to jump in, but everyone was hesitant when they felt the frigid pool water. Thankfully, the alcohol gave Max enough courage to jump in. As he shivered, he realized he needed to stop trying to impress Lee. But when Lee leapt in, they had so much fun swimming together. Max was torn between guilt and excitement. The alcohol was blurring that line by the minute, but Max kept saying yes whenever Lee offered him a drink.

It didn't take long for everyone to head inside. Once Max suggested that a hot shower sounded amazing, everyone else thought so too. Instead of taking turns, they all got in at once while wearing their trunks and two pieces. Max had never been in such a wild situation with such crazy people, but he didn't object out of fear he would be made fun of. It made him feel excited. Max had a blast during the goofy shaving cream fights that followed.

Slowly, people got out of the shower. Max and Lee refused to get out, leaving them alone together. They shared a couple of nervous giggles. Lee began soaping Max's bare chest as Max's excitement returned down below. He hoped Lee didn't notice. How embarrassing would that be?

"Someone is easily aroused!" Lee did notice.

"You know, I had hoped the first time I showered with a guy, he would be single." Max spoke up, ignoring Lee's prior comment out of pure embarrassment.

"If this is your first time in a shower with a guy, you need to be naked!" Lee said, teasingly.

They smiled at each other, but Max decided it was time to get out and not jeopardize his heart. Max had to win his battle against making a move with Lee. They dried off and joined their friends for a movie. Not far into *The Human Centipede*, Lee put his feet on Max's lap. Max couldn't help thinking about how good and natural that felt to him, much more natural than what was happening on the T.V.

After the movie ended, Lee decided he wanted to go play ping pong in the rec room. Max agreed, and on the way there he got a mischievous idea. Max suggested they play strip ping pong. The alcohol and horniness was clearly making its way to his head. He told Lee that they should take an article of clothing off every time they missed the ball. To Max's pleasant surprise, Lee agreed.

Max's mind bounced back and forth like the ping pong ball, jumping between right and wrong. He really liked Lee, but they couldn't be together. Max wanted to steal him away, but that would be wrong. Max wanted to let him be his first kiss, but that would be cheating. Back and forth his mind traveled between right and wrong.

Lee dropped his pants for a millisecond then rushed them back on after missing the ball for the fifth time. Max caught a glimpse of Lee's dark red briefs. He teased Lee for being a total chicken. The rest of the group soon joined in the rec room. They all had so much fun together. The natural flow between Max and Lee was indescribable. Max already felt like they were boyfriends.

The rest of the night consisted of a late night grocery trip and Max and Lee singing Justin Bieber's *Baby* at Waffle House. Confusion struck Max as he watched Lee openly flirt with him in front of Lee's other friends. What were Lee's friends thinking? Did they see him as someone who wanted to sabotage Lee's love life? He didn't want that label even if it meant he could have Lee right then and there.

Around one o'clock in the morning they got back to their cars. After everyone left, Lee said, "I guess this is the part where I kiss you good night."

"It would be if you were single!" Max seemed to have to remind him all night.

"At least hang out with me in my car for a bit. I don't want to leave," Lee said, begging.

Against his better judgment, Max gave in. When Max got into Lee's car, he felt as if he was giving into Lee. They sat in his car, turned on some music, and talked the rest of the night away. Lee learned how Max had never kissed a boy, and Lee took that as a challenge. He was clearly still tipsy. When Max shot him down, Lee convinced Max to cuddle in the back seat of the car. Max was angry at himself at first, but once Lee held him, the anger vanished.

Flooded with fear and comfort, Max lay in Lee's arms. *Gravity* by Sara Bareilles was playing on the radio. Max felt so amazing, but he didn't want to end up hurt. With teary eyes, he told Lee about the sadness he constantly felt. He explained how coming out didn't take that pain away like he thought it would. He also told him that his friend Tyler had abandoned him. If Lee hurt him also, he wasn't sure he could survive it.

Max sat up and put his hand on the door handle to exit the car.

"Wait, just kiss me before you go! I don't know what will happen with my boyfriend, but I like you." Lee stopped him from leaving.

"I can't!" Max stood his ground.

"Just come here."

"But I can't!" Max insisted.

"Just come here," Lee whispered with his hand on Max's face.

"I ca-"

"Come here," Lee said for the last time as Max gave in and leaned forward into Lee's lips. Max's heart stopped, and time seemed to freeze in that moment. Excitement and bliss consumed Max.

Max drove home that night with so many unanswered questions. Would Lee leave his long distance boyfriend? Would Max end up being abandoned again? What would Max's friends think of him going after somebody who was taken? Although he had no idea what the future held, he pulled into his driveway with a smile on his face. He placed his fingers on his lips where Lee's lips had just been, and he smiled.

Chapter 12

Fifteen months before coming out...

"Did you hear Nick finally admitted he was gay?" Tyler asked Max while hanging out with him at the community pool. "I mean it was totally obvious with that voice of his."

Max wasn't sure how to respond. He had pretty much pushed the gay issue into the back of his mind and only wanted to enjoy his summer. "Oh, wow. That's crazy. We should probably start praying for the poor guy during Bible studies," Max suggested.

"So, you think it's a sin?" Tyler kept the conversation going.

"It says so in the Bible. Plain and simple." Max answered with confidence.

They let the conversation drop there, and they went to jump in the pool. Max cursed himself every time he checked out a guy's bare chest. It was especially hard on him when he could see an outline of what the boys had in their trunks. He'd been fighting so hard to ignore his lust, but the pool was making it difficult. He forced himself to look at girls' boobs, hoping it would help.

All night long, Max could not get his mind off of Nick and his news. Max knew the emotion he felt. He hated to admit it, but he was jealous. Nick would get to do what Max dreamed about. *If only I didn't care about going to Heaven,* he thought. Max figured this was the devil's way of getting to him.

Max opened up his laptop and went to Facebook. Nick's page had a new post about him coming out. The comment section was full of love and support. How could so many people be ok with this perverse sin? Confusion overwhelmed Max. He thought he was making the right choice to fight his desires, but the support Nick was getting looked appealing.

Curious, Max clicked to send Nick a private message. Although he just wanted to discuss the topic of homosexuality, he didn't want Nick to suspect anything, so he made the message into a letter of concern. He told Nick that he didn't have to choose to be gay. Max clicked send and awaited Nick's response.

Not even two minutes later, a message from Nick appeared. "I appreciate your concern, but I'm fine the way I am!"

The smug response infuriated Max. How could Nick be so confident in something so wrong? Max wrote him back, informing him that he was just trying to help. He decided to just let it go and pray for Nick that night. Unfortunately, Nick wasn't going to drop it.

"I know you better than you think." Nick wrote. "You're

hiding your sexuality and covering it up with religion. You didn't expect me to think you were straight did you? Why else would you be so concerned with my life?"

That little bastard, Max thought before responding. "Listen here! Your messed up life is your decision! I'm not going to argue with a gay guy who doesn't realize what he's doing!" He slammed his finger on the send key. He shut his laptop and slung himself on his bed. He placed a pillow over his head and screamed. Before long, tears formed in his eyes. He prayed to God to free him from his pain, and he drifted off to sleep.

Max was glad to be relaxed the next morning. It helped him deal with yet another message from Nick. Nick apologized for automatically assuming he was gay. He told Max he was a little on edge last night due to some hate mail he got on Facebook. Max was shocked when he got to the bottom of the message and saw Nick had invited him to hang out and chat.

No matter how many times Max told himself it was a bad idea, he couldn't convince himself to not talk to Nick. He had to know what it was like for Nick to be so open and honest. That day, they met at A Pizza Paradise to talk. Max's anxiety was unbearable at the thought that someone would see them together. Thank God the place wasn't crowded.

"So, why are you so concerned with my sexuality?" Nick asked in his high, effeminate voice.

"Uh... I was just trying to help and tell you there was hope. You don't have to go against God." Max's voice shook.

"Did it occur to you that I may not believe in God? Come on, I know there's more to it!" Nick bit into his pizza waiting for Max to respond.

Before he knew it, Max was telling Nick the truth about his struggles. He made Nick swear not to say a word to anyone. He informed Nick about his faith journey and how he didn't want to hurt God or his family. He wanted to be normal and just live his life, and he didn't believe he could do that as a gay guy.

"Ok cutie, listen here. If there is a God, he's not going to throw you in Hell for loving another man. Nothing can change how you feel. You'll be better off when you accept that!" Sass radiated off of Nick when he spoke.

Max ignored the remark about him being cute and continued telling Nick that he refused to live that life. Deep down he kind of wanted to live like Nick though. He seemed so care free. Would it be possible to be gay and content in life at the same time? Max wasn't sure he could be convinced.

After going back and forth arguing about the topic of homosexuality while eating their pizza, they went their separate ways. It was as if the conversation went nowhere because neither of them were willing to budge on their views. To get his mind off of everything, Max went home and practiced playing his saxophone. With every note, he pushed away his conversation with Nick.

At ten o'clock that night, Max's phone buzzed. Nick must have gotten his number off of Facebook. He politely thanked Max for the talk that day and wished him a good night. Max wondered why he was being so nice? After all, he didn't agree with Nick's lifestyle. It didn't take him long to guess that Nick was crushing on him.

When his phoned buzzed again, his jaw dropped open when he saw what was on his screen. Right before his eyes was a picture of Nick's penis. *What the fuck?* Max was confused, but also turned on. This made his blood boil. Why was Nick torturing him like this?

"What the hell, man?" Max responded with adrenaline pumping through his veins.

"You know you like it! Now show me yours!" Nick typed back.

All of Max's morals were being taken over by his excessive horniness. Before he knew it, he was taking off his pants and snapping a picture of his goods. His finger shook as he hit send. He couldn't believe what he had just done! It didn't take long for Nick to respond, talking about the things he wanted to do with Max.

After Max finished sexting, he lay in a bed of guilt. He felt desperately sick to his stomach about what had just taken place. He was angry at himself and at Nick. *What the fuck is wrong with me?* Tears began pouring down his face as he asked for God's forgiveness. He felt nothing but hatred towards himself. He began to think, for the first time, that he would be better off dead.

Chapter 13

Two hours had passed since Max's last text from Lee, and he was going crazy. Why wasn't he texting Max back? Was he with his boyfriend? Lee hadn't mentioned seeing him today. Maybe Lee decided he was done with Max for good. Max's heart dropped at the thought. He began to wish he had never gone to that party when his phone finally buzzed.

Max jumped up and down in his room when Lee invited him to hang out with his friends again. He was determined to make Lee see that he was better for him than his current boyfriend. There was far too much chemistry there to just let it go with the wind. Lee was worth the chase.

Again, Max took forever to get ready, trying to find the perfect outfit. He settled on a pink polo and black pants. He ran gel through his hair until it was just right. He spent more time than usual brushing his teeth, thinking about Lee tasting his lips and tongue.

When Max ran downstairs, his father stopped him. He got drilled with questions about where he was going. Ever since coming out, his dad seemed more and more unhappy with him. He claimed he was trying to understand, but he always seemed bothered. This frustrated Max. His dad would never know how hard he tried to impress him.

"I don't know these people you are hanging out with!" Max's dad said.

"Is there a problem with you not knowing who all my friends are? It never mattered before," Max said, grunting.

"I just want you to be safe," his dad responded.

"I think you mean straight!" Max said as he walked out the door.

Everyone met up for buffalo wings that evening. While Lee's friends chatted it up, Max and Lee stayed in their own world. Lee began rubbing his foot up and down Max's leg. Chills went up and down Max's spine with the slightest touch. They smiled, laughed, and got to know each other even more throughout that dinner.

"I dare you to try their hottest sauce!" Lee said, challenging Max.

"You're on!" Max really didn't want to, but his better judgment vanished when he was around Lee and his friends.

Five boneless chicken wings came out, covered in a fiery red sauce. They smelled just like a hot chili pepper. Max began to sweat just looking at them. Everyone at the table stared at him, waiting to see if he had the balls to go through with the challenge. Max put a piece of chicken on his fork and shoved it in his mouth.

"It's not that bad." Max chewed on the chicken.

Suddenly, his tongue felt like it was on fire. Huge beads

of sweat poured down his face. He felt as if he was going to die! He looked at Lee with a panicked face. Lee handed him his water, and Max drank the whole glass. It took another twenty minutes for him to cool down.

"I'm impressed!" Lee said.

Max was curious as to what his limitations were when it came to making Lee like him. Sadly, there weren't a lot of things Max wouldn't do. He knew it wasn't healthy to do reckless things for a boy, but Lee's charm was worth it all to Max. He was hoping Lee would choose him, even if he didn't do crazy things for his love. By now, Lee was bound to know that Max would go to great lengths for him.

On the way out of the restaurant, Lee stopped Max and let his friends go out. Max gave a puzzled look, not knowing why Lee stopped him. Then, Lee pulled Max in close for another kiss. Lee's lips tasted like honey barbecue. Max didn't want the kiss to end, but Lee pulled away. Lee held Max's hand until they got out of the restaurant and were back with the group. When Lee let go of his hand, a sorrowful feeling overwhelmed Max.

Lee liked to make Max feel special then he would do something to remind him that they weren't actually together. Max wasn't even sure if Lee was aware of what he was doing to Max's fragile emotions. Max wanted to be able to hold Lee's hand in front of anyone, but their affections towards each other had to be hidden. Max couldn't live like that much longer.

When they arrived at the college apartment complex, they began setting up for a party. Lee had a DJ friend who was going to come and drop some sick beats. They filled the fridge with alcohol and pushed the couches together to make room for a dance floor. Max had to fight through the sexual tension with Lee just to get the place set up.

The couches were scooted to the edge of the room, leaving plenty of space for a dance floor. Party lights were placed in the corner, aiming towards the center of the floor. A drink table was set up by the kitchen, just a few feet from the beer pong table.

Max considered inviting his friends, but he didn't want to be judged for going after a guy who was taken. Max needed them to break up first. Wouldn't Lee want to leave his boyfriend? Why would he make the moves he was making if he didn't want to leave his long distance man? Max decided he would have to talk to him about this dilemma that night.

When the party started, Max and Lee faced off in beer pong. It was Max's first time playing, so it didn't take long for him to get down to just three cups left. Miraculously, Max made his next four shots, and Lee drank accordingly. After Max lost, he went and opened a fruity drink to make up for the nasty beer taste.

The beer was flowing and the music was bouncing by around eleven o'clock. A wildly diverse group of people were dancing and making out on the dance floor. Two girls were grinding all over one another, one of them with her hands down the other's pants. It looked like a toned down orgy to Max. Slowly, the party became a blurry mass of dancing bodies. Max was getting a bit too tipsy, and it wasn't even midnight yet.

He stumbled over to Lee and told him they needed to have a little chat. Lee followed Max into a nearby bedroom, but before Max could begin to talk, Lee pushed him to the bed and got on top of him. They began making out and letting their hands wander all over each other. Max was in heaven.

Lee's hands made it down to Max's pants buttons. He began to unbutton them when Max grabbed his hand. Lee looked up at Max as if to ask why Max stopped him. Max rolled Lee off of him and got out of the bed. He nearly fell over while trying to catch his breath in an attempt to handle the effect of the alcohol.

"We need to talk. I think I love you, but you're still with someone else!" Max blurted out, shocked he had said the "L" word.

Guilt covered Lee's face as he responded. "I know this isn't fair to you. I love Vick, but I'm having an amazing time with you."

It was the first time Max had heard the guy's name. It felt like a sting to the heart. Was Lee saying he didn't want to leave Vick? Max's head was spinning. He began to get very nauseous. He ran out of the bedroom and into the bathroom to throw up. He locked the door to the bathroom, sat on the floor, and started to cry.

"Let me in, man!" Lee's voice came from outside the door.

"Leave me alone. I should have never met you!" Max screamed, not caring who heard.

A few minutes later, a piece of paper slid underneath the

door. Rolling his eyes, Max began to read what was written on it. More tears began falling as he read, "I can't stay away from your gravity. It keeps pulling at me. Just have some more fun with me, please."

Max knew why he chose those words. It was all because of the song, *Gravity,* that was playing in the car when they first kissed. How did Lee know exactly what to say to get Max to fall for him over and over again? He got up and left the bathroom. He was still mesmerized by Lee's beautiful face. He chose to accept that Lee was torn, and he chose to try not to care about it.

Lee went up to the DJ and whispered something in his ear. As Lee walked back to Max, the four piano chords from *Gravity* played. Although other people seemed annoyed by the change of tempo to a slow song, Lee didn't care. Lee grabbed Max and began dancing with him. Lee had his hands around Max's waist, and he pulled him close. Max gulped, nervously worrying about what Lee's friends were thinking.

Lee somehow knew what Max was thinking. "I don't care what anyone else thinks! This is what I want right now!" Lee smiled, flashing his perfect teeth.

Those words made Max's face turn red. He was blushing harder than he ever had before. Suddenly, it felt like they were the only ones on the dance floor. Max wanted to stay in that moment forever.

"I'll leave him," Lee whispered as he leaned in and kissed Max. This time, Max didn't pull back. They kissed for what felt like five minutes. Those minutes could've turned into hours, days, weeks, months, or years. Max wouldn't have minded one bit. He was happy.

Once he was sobered up, Max said goodbye and drove home. It was around three in the morning when he quietly opened his house door. He made it halfway up the steps before his dad called his name. He had been sitting in his recliner, waiting for him to get home.

"We've been too lenient on you, Max," his dad said sternly.

"You never said when I had to be home." Max defended himself.

"Well, you've never been out this late in the past!" His dad's voice began to raise.

"Ok, you're just upset because I was with a guy! You wouldn't give a shit if I was with some girl! I tried living that life for you! I'm sorry I'm not your perfect son!" Max said, his voice raising higher, then he stormed to his room.

Max lay in bed fighting back tears. He just wanted to be able to stay happy for a full twenty-four hours. Something always had to bring him down. He started to think he spent more time feeling sad than being content. He put his headphones on, played *Gravity,* and fell asleep thinking about Lee.

Chapter 14

One year before coming out...

Max did everything he could to avoid Nick when school started. Nick got the hint and left him alone for the most part. Only on occasion would Nick send him a message telling Max that he should accept himself. To Max, he had done just that. He accepted himself as a strong Christian man who wouldn't give in to sin. He had even started to help with the middle schoolers at the church.

He had an absolute blast with the kids. They were always full of energy and questions. Max had to make sure he was all studied up on his Bible so that he could guide them correctly. He never would have imagined he would have such a heart for kids. He was so happy Ryan had asked him to help out.

One of the kids asked him, "Was there really a talking snake?"

"There's a lot of crazy things that happened in biblical days, so it's possible! It would be pretty cool, wouldn't it?"

Max answered the boy, who reminded him a lot of his brother, Cole.

Cole had one more year until he would be in with the middle schoolers at church. Max was hoping he could completely take over the middle school youth program by then. He knew Ryan couldn't handle everything on his plate, so he would train to take his place with the middle schoolers. Ryan enjoyed working with high schoolers more anyway. He had told Max that he was getting too old to deal with the energy levels that the youngsters had.

Friday at school, Max welcomed Tyler back. Tyler had been out of town for a family emergency. During his absence, Max made friends with Jess and Adrianna. They were peppy cheerleaders with hearts of gold. Tyler was happy to have more friends to sit with at the lunch table, and he felt good about the fact that they were cheerleaders. He figured he could use the cool points.

When asked about his family emergency, Tyler didn't want to talk about it. His eyes watered at the mention of it. Max wished he would open up about everything, but every time he asked about it, Tyler changed the subject to pointless banter. All Max could do was pray for Tyler and his family. Maybe one day Tyler would let him in.

"I really don't know what's going on with him!" Max told Ryan over coffee.

"He hasn't opened up to me either, but I'm sure he will when he's ready," Ryan responded. "Let's get back to you. How has the temptation been?"

"Well, it's been normal. I can't seem to keep away from

porn. I've chosen to believe prayer will take it away, but it's not." Max put his head down. He felt defeated.

"I've been doing my own research. Unfortunately, what I have found is that most ex-gay Christians never get rid of their desires. They just fight through it." Ryan knew it wasn't the news Max wanted.

"Oh, great!" Max buried his head in his hands. "This isn't fair. I'm going to be miserable forever!"

"No, you won't. My best advice is to surround yourself with good guy friends, like Tyler, and spend some time with your dad. The more male influences, the better!" Ryan responded with hope in his voice.

Max liked Ryan's idea to spend more time with the men in his life. After Max's dad picked him up from the coffee shop, he decided to take some initiative. "Dad, would you want to spend the day together tomorrow? Maybe we can take Cole out for some ice cream and go to the park or something?"

A smile spread across his dad's face as he said, "Of course! There's actually a go-kart place that just opened up. We can go there after ice cream."

The next day, Max, Cole, and their father got ready and headed off to *Cold Stone Creamery* for some ice cream. Laughs quickly rose to the surface as Cole covered his face in vanilla ice cream. Max had to take a picture of his adorable little brother. Cole wanted to keep the mess on his face as a reminder of the amazing ice cream he just had.

"Can I have another? Please?" Cole begged his dad for more ice cream.

"You're already gonna have enough energy!" Max ruffled his fingers through Cole's hair as he pouted.

Cole's face lit up like a Christmas tree when he saw the go-kart course. Even though Max was a junior in high school, he still was thrilled to be there. Heck, even his dad had a mischievous smile on his face. Nothing could stop the Stevenson boys! There was, however, one problem.

"Cole, you're gonna have to ride with me. You're not old enough yet," Max's dad informed his obviously disappointed younger brother.

"No! I'm close enough to twelve!" Cole begged his dad to let him drive.

"Ride with me, and I promise we will beat Dad!" Max spoke up to calm him down. Cole nodded his head in agreement.

"How has your time been with Ryan?" his dad asked while waiting in line.

"Well, it's been good. I think I want to take over the middle school youth when I'm ready," Max responded, leaving out the homosexuality issue.

"I'm really proud of you, son! You've become a fine young man, and I admire your pursuit of Christ." His dad smiled.

Everyone had such positive vibes that day. Max needed that more than anything, a break from stress and a break from his own mind. Max and Cole zoomed around a corner and passed their father. They beat him on the final stretch. Cole threw his fists in the air in victorious celebration. Max thanked God that Ryan gave him the suggestion to spend time with them.

Cole quickly zonked out on the way back home. Max and his dad talked about church and school and everything else going on in Max's life. It eventually got difficult to navigate the waters of Max's life without getting into sexuality issues. It was such a huge part of Max's mind. He wished he could confide in his dad, but he refused to ruin the good mood he was in.

Back at school, Tyler began to return to normal. Max could never figure out what had happened, but he wasn't going to pry. After Max told Tyler all about the go-karts, they agreed to go together sometime. Tyler suggested inviting the girls. Max figured Tyler had a crush on one of them. They were very pretty, after all.

One night, after Max finished his homework, another text came in from Nick. Max let out a huge sigh as he opened it up. Nick apologized for initiating sending the naughty pictures. He wanted Max to know that wasn't what it meant to be gay. He was sad that Max had to live in the closet, and he really wanted to help him.

Max rolled his eyes, put his phone on his desk, and said, "Not today, Satan!"

Chapter 15

"He's absolutely perfect!" Max raved on and on about Lee. He was finally catching up with Jess, Adrianna, and Joseph. There was little time left for them after Lee broke up with his boyfriend. Strangely, Lee hadn't made anything official with Max. *Nothing wrong with taking it slow,* Max thought.

"Well, I'm not a fan of him because he's taken you away from us! We've missed you. Talking at school just isn't enough," Jess responded while guiding the group into her favorite clothing store.

"I agree. I've gotten pretty fond of you, man! We have got to hang out more!" Joseph said while giving Max a little punch on the shoulder. Max considered that to be such a bro move.

Max knew he was flaking on his friends a lot, but he couldn't pull himself away from Lee. They could sit in a quiet room together, and Max would be one hundred percent satisfied. He didn't care just how pathetic that seemed. Lee was more compelling than Max had expected him to be.

"I will make you guys meet him one day!" Max held up a nice shirt to see how good he would look in it. After deciding it wasn't Lee's style, he put it back up.

"Babe, you've been awful quiet. Is everything ok?" Joseph asked Adrianna while rubbing her back for comfort. She hadn't said a word all day.

Then, like a burst pipe, everything spilled out. She ranted about her failing grade in math class. She tried studying, but she could never get anywhere. She wanted to get into a good college, but she was losing faith in herself. She told everyone she was just as disappointed in herself as her parents were.

"I had no idea!" Joseph responded with a genuine concern that calmed Adrianna down in an instant. It was as if he was some super boyfriend. Max began to wonder if Joseph had any flaws at all. Adrianna rested her head on his shoulder and smiled.

Joseph went on to tell everyone a story about his father in the army. "When someone was in trouble," he said, "they would yell out the words 'broken arrow'. This was the signal that informed the team to run to the rescue. They wouldn't leave anyone behind."

"This is very random, honey," Adrianna said, chuckling.

"No, it really isn't. We are all friends here, and you need our support. Whenever any one of us is struggling, we should just text the words 'broken arrow' and we will know to come save the day." He spoke with a heroic heart.

Max admired Joseph so much for that moment. He thought about the times he could have used a support team to come and rescue him. Max felt at ease around Joseph, so he made a mental note to start including him in his life more. He added him under the favorites section of his phone, right below Lee.

Later that night, Max got dressed up to go hang out with Lee. Max began showing his excitement in his pants, just at the thought of kissing Lee. He figured it might be time for him to go a little further with Lee. That would take care of his excitement. Max adjusted himself to hide his boner.

"When do I get to meet this special guy?" Max's mom asked.

"Whenever I'm ready for you to!" Max responded with a smirk.

His mom shook her head and gave Max a kiss on the forehead. Max's dad sat on the recliner with a disturbed look on his face. It still hurt Max to see his father's disapproval. He tried his best to ignore it and focus on his mother's unconditional love, but he couldn't seem to shake the hurt he felt for disappointing his dad.

Max turned his music up loud as he drove over to Lee's house. He let the sounds of Troye Sivan drown out the image of his disapproving father. Thinking about Troye's good looks was enough to lift Max's spirits. Ever since Troye popped up on the radio, Max became obsessed with his music style. Troye kept Max company up until he made it to Lee's.

Max's heart raced as his hands shook. He knocked on Lee's apartment door and waited for him to open it. Max was convinced he had never seen so much beauty at once. Lee wore a thin leather jacket that hugged his body, showing every curve around his muscles. To match the tight jacket, his skinny jeans didn't leave much to the imagination. Immediately, Max went in for a kiss. Lee had to pull away after a few minutes and remind Max that he had cooked dinner.

They ate a delicious spaghetti that Lee had prepared from scratch as they talked about life. Lee seemed to show a lot of interest in meeting Max's friends, which thrilled Max. Max felt kind of bad for not getting close to Lee's friends. Honestly, he couldn't even remember their names. He put too much focus on Lee. One day he would make an effort with them.

After dinner they sat on the couch, and Lee turned on Netflix. Max's hand ventured down to Lee's crotch as they began kissing. Max was shocked by how adventurous he had become after sharing his first kiss with Lee. It was like Max became a completely different person, and he loved it. Feeling the excitement in Lee's pants made Max's heart beat out of his chest. He unbuttoned Lee's pants and pulled them down. Lee did the same for Max.

Before they knew it, they were heavily making out in their underwear. Max had never felt so good, yet scared, in his entire life. He wanted Lee with every nerve in his body. He squeezed Lee closer to him, never wanting to let go. He wanted time to freeze. Lee had become an addiction.

"Stop!" Lee shouted while Max tried to take off his underwear.

"Don't you want to have sex with me?" Max questioned, feeling a little hurt.

"Of course! You're adorable, but now isn't the best time." Lee was trying to let Max down gently.

Afraid to dig any further, Max let it go, although he wanted to cry because of the rejection. They continued watching T.V. Lee nearly fell asleep on Max's shoulder. He eventually raised up and reminded Max that he should probably head home. Max had texted Lee earlier about his fight with his dad. He didn't want Max to have to go through a repeat.

Max was relieved to see his mother when he returned home. His dad must have already knocked out for the night. Max stopped in his tracks when he realized his mother had been crying. He hoped and prayed that the tears weren't his fault. He hated seeing his mother sad. When she hurt, he hurt too.

"What happened? You ok?" Max asked his distraught mother.

"I'm fine, sweetie. Just trying to help your father understand that you can't help the way you are. He thinks I'm too soft on you," his mom said, laughing. "He'll come around."

Hearing his mother laugh relaxed Max. He always felt a sense of joy when his mom was happy. Max often thought about how he would sacrifice his own happiness to make sure his mom was content, but thankfully he didn't have to do that. His mom would never allow it.

"What if he never understands?" Max was getting extremely aggravated at his father.

"If he can't learn to accept it, then he is going to miss out on a lot!" His mom kissed him on the forehead.

Although it was his father that made his mother cry, Max couldn't help but feel guilty. If there was a magic pill that could turn Max straight, he would take it. Life would be so much easier. He'd have his father's approval, Tyler would still be his friend, and he'd never have to fear being judged. Max went to bed that night, dreaming of a life where he liked women.

Chapter 16

Ten months before coming out...

It was like a prayer had finally been answered. Pure Hope Counseling, the organization Max contacted a while back, was now offering a free support group. There wouldn't be a licensed counselor there, but there would be people who were wearing the same shoes as Max. A nervous excitement pulsed through Max's veins.

A friendly voice spoke when Max stepped into the counseling office, "Howdy, how are you?"

Max shyly introduced himself and asked where he was supposed to go for the group. The gray-haired man with piercings in his ears led Max into a room full of guys sitting in a circle. Max felt like an alcoholic at an AA meeting. It made him uncomfortable that he was the youngest guy there.

The group started out with a prayer led by George, the guy who first introduced himself to Max at the front desk. Max rubbed his sweaty palms together as he glanced around at the men in the room. They all had this sadness that seemed to hover over them. It was a sorrow that Max knew all too well. He wondered if this would be his fate. Would he be sitting in this group forty years from now, still crying over his unwanted attractions?

After prayer, the group put on a video. A very butch man stood in front of a tool table and spoke about being a man. He stressed the importance of sports, building things, and fixing things. It was as if he was saying that doing these things would cure homosexuality. Max knew better than to believe all men had to be that way, and he sure as hell knew that wasn't going to make him like boobs.

The whole class seemed a little ridiculous. He sat and listened to these men talk about forced relations with women. It all came off as extremely hopeless. So much for Pure Hope Counseling. Max was pretty sure he would never return to that group again. The group put a bad taste in his mouth and set his mind on a totally unexpected path.

He started to realize he would never feel for women what he felt for men. He refused to be an old man, still fighting to force himself to like women. What did that discovery mean for Max? He still didn't think he could be with men. Perhaps his only option would be to vow to be celibate. Maybe it's what God wanted for him all along.

Max thought about the many horny nights he spent alone in his room. Could he handle living like that for the rest of his life? He was willing to do whatever God asked of him, but how much would he have to give up? He wished that God would give him a sign in his moment of desperation.

BUZZ! BUZZ! Max's phone alerted him to a text

message. He grunted as he saw a message from Nick. Nick wanted to get together and talk more about Max's attractions. It would be a while longer before Ryan picked him up from the group, and, after all, he was right beside a burger joint. Max reluctantly asked Nick to meet him for a bite to eat. He quietly snuck out of the group and headed across the road.

"Hey hey hey! How's it hanging?" Nick bounced in and sat down at the table Max was holding for them.

"Hi. I'm alright," Max responded rather coldly, remembering the pictures they had sent to each other.

"Perk up, buttercup!" Nick snapped. His sassiness was overwhelming.

Max told Nick all about the depressing group he had just attended. Nick laughed harder than he should have, considering the restaurant was dead quiet. Max's face turned red as he looked around to see if anyone was staring. If someone he knew saw him, he would have a lot of explaining to do.

"Daaaaaaamn, he's cute!" Nick raved about their waiter after he left to get their drinks.

Max thought he was attractive as well, but he could not bring himself to admit such a thing. "How are you so ok with being gay in this world that is so against us... I mean you?" Max corrected himself so that he wasn't including himself under the gay label.

"Screw society! If we lived trying to please everyone, we would go crazy! I promise you'll be much happier when you come out!" Nick smiled.

"I'm not coming out. It may be ok for you, but not me.

I'll probably remain celibate for my whole life!" Max regretted sounding sad about celibacy, because he knew it would give Nick more ammo against him being in the closet.

"You know, I'm sad for you!" Nick winked at the waiter, then returned to Max. "There is so much happiness to be found on the other side of the closet door! You're really going to damage yourself if you keep fighting it like this!"

Max knew it was taking a toll on his mental state, but sometimes God asks a lot of his followers. He found himself slipping and thinking about what life would be like if he did come out. A slight feeling of joy crept inside his mind. *Snap out of it!* Max hated himself for even giving it a thought.

"Why do you talk to me if you don't want to come out?" Nick questioned.

"Well, you're the only person my age that knows what I'm going through. You're my only outlet," Max answered.

"Bullshit! I call total bullshit! I know you want to come out and accept yourself for the dick lover that you are! It may be tomorrow, or it may be a year from now, but I will convince you of what you already want to be convinced of!" Nick was full of an arrogance that annoyed Max, yet Max somehow envied Nick. He had a sense of confidence that Max thought he would never have.

After Max chowed down on an amazing burger and fries, Ryan swung by to pick him up. Max hopped in the car and sat quietly for most of the ride home. What was he supposed to tell Ryan? He thought the group was total bullshit. The only thing Max felt certain of was the fact that he was far more intrigued by Nick's life than he was by the lives of the depressed older men.

Chapter 17

Max stared at the ceiling for thirty minutes after waking up on a Saturday morning. A heavy sense of sorrow weighed him down to the point that he could not leave his bed. His parents were out of the house working, and Cole was over at a friend's house. No matter how many positive things Max thought about, he still could not rise out of his funk.

He imagined Lee climbing into bed with him to cheer him up. He wanted to tell Lee how hurt he was over how certain people had handled him coming out. He needed to rant about how he had thought coming out would be his answer to happiness, but it had been far from it. However, there was no way to tell Lee his troubles if Lee wouldn't respond to his texts or phone calls.

Max was stuck in an endless cycle. He couldn't get up because he was feeling low, but he felt even lower because he couldn't get up. He thought about texting "broken arrow" to his friends, but he wouldn't even know how to explain how he felt. He needed a reason to get out of the house. He wanted to spend time with Tyler.

There were many complicated feelings Max was experiencing towards Tyler. He was sad that Tyler no longer wanted to be friends. He was afraid there was nothing he could do about that. He was angry that Tyler would react like he did. Max knew Tyler well enough to know it was far more than a religion thing. His reaction was very out of character.

Max decided to take his dog, Cooper, for a walk. He needed the fresh air and rays of sunshine. Still, Max found himself beyond frustrated every time Cooper stopped to smell a flower. He wanted to yank the dog's chain in frustration, but he couldn't hurt Cooper. *Why can't I control my emotions?* Max was tired of feeling out of control.

When he returned home, he opened up his laptop and headed to a website called *Tumblr*. Adrianna had talked about how all kinds of people from different walks of life would blog about any topic imaginable there. Max figured he would see what kind of emotional struggles others were going through.

He typed the word *depressed* in the search bar and awaited the results. He wasn't convinced that he was a clinically depressed people who needed medication. He felt he was emotionally depressed but not chemically imbalanced. He had to try and fix his life, one problem at a time. Surely that couldn't be too hard.

A message in all capital letters popped up on Max's screen. "Feeling suicidal? Get help now!" The message had a number for a suicide hotline. Max promised himself he would never sink that low. He wasn't that bad off. However, every depressing post that followed felt like it was coming from Max's heart.

Immediately, Max made his own account and titled it "Broken Arrow." He began to reblog quotes and photos that represented the pain he was feeling on a daily basis. Only during rare moments with Lee, Jess, Adrianna, or Joseph, did he feel at ease. That day, Max didn't have the strength to reach out, so he was left alone with his blog and his thoughts.

Before he knew it, Max's parents arrived home with Cole. Max slammed his laptop shut and went downstairs. It was a relief to be around other humans again. His mom gave him a concerned look when she saw Max's red, puffy face. "I'm ok," Max mouthed at his mom to ease her mind. He just wished he could be convinced of that, too.

For dinner that night, they had lasagna. Max absolutely loved his mother's lasagna recipe. It had a slight spice to it that wowed Max's taste buds. Cole could only handle so much of it before gulping down an entire glass of water. Max liked to tease him for being a wimp.

"I'm not a wimp!" Cole shouted as he shoved another bite of lasagna into his little mouth.

Max waited, with a mischievous grin, for Cole to react to the huge bite he had swallowed. Sweat drops poured down Cole's face as he turned slightly red. Cole gripped the arm chair and stared Max in the eyes. *Three...Two...One...* Max counted down. As soon as he hit one, Cole ran into the bathroom for more water. The whole family laughed, and Max finally had a small moment where he could smile.

"Bub, I think I'm going to be gay like you when I grow up," Cole said, looking proudly at his older brother.

Fuck! Max knew his brief moment of happiness was about to get tense. He glanced at his dad who looked as if he had just been shot in the heart. Surely Cole had no idea what he was talking about! There was no way in hell he could be gay too. His dad got up and excused himself from the table as his mom gave her husband a menacing look.

"If that's what you feel like you want when it's time for you to date, then that's ok!" His mom said, comforting Cole. Honestly, her voice comforted Max, too.

"There's no way you can know yet!" Max said loud enough for his dad to hear. He knew what he said was bullshit, because he definitely had found guys attractive at Cole's age.

Max was all for Cole being himself, but he wouldn't wish the hardships of being gay on anyone. Max was convinced it was just something Cole said because he had witnessed his brother come out. Still, with every word about being gay, Max's father grew farther and farther from the family. Max could tell it was taking a toll on his mother.

"Where do you think that came from?" Max asked his mom while helping her with the dishes.

"I'm less concerned about that and more concerned with how your father is treating his family," his mom responded in frustration. "I'm going to make him go to counseling with me."

"Things are that serious?" Max was shocked.

"Of course they are. Your father is treating you like a second class citizen, and he'll do the same thing to Cole if he isn't straight!" Max's mother was getting heated.

Max couldn't help but place some blame on himself for his parents' problems. If he had never come out, their marriage would be just fine. Instead, Max felt like every harsh word and every glare were his fault. He began to miss the days before he came out. So that his mother wouldn't see him cry, Max rushed up the stairs and went to his bedroom.

Max reopened his laptop and headed to the *Tumblr* online community. The rest of the night, he scrolled through pictures, stories, quotes, and GIFs representing people's depression. It all resonated way too deeply with Max. Although he wasn't feeling very close to God, he prayed, asking God not to allow him to be depressed. Being gay was enough for anyone to deal with, and he didn't need mental illness to pile on top of that.

In a short time, *Tumblr* became an addiction for Max. If he wasn't on the desktop site, he had it pulled up on his iPhone. Max was fascinated by other people's honesty when it came to how they were feeling. So many people his age talked about killing themselves, and that broke Max's heart to witness.

He wrote a few of these people and tried to convince them that life was worth living. He wanted to be a light in their lives. Surely, he would be able to make them understand that there is beauty in the world. While pushing his point, he discovered something unpleasant. Max was more convinced by what the suicidal people thought about life than what he was trying to tell them.

Chapter 18

Eight months before coming out...

It was the day of Max and Tyler's first band concert of the year. Max was struggling to tie his bow tie. Thankfully his dad came to the rescue and taught him how to tie it the correct way. When Max was finished getting ready, he looked in the mirror and felt like the sharpest man around.

"You look so handsome, sweetie!" his mom said while dusting off the shoulders of Max's suit.

Max was quite nervous because this would be his first saxophone solo in front of a crowd. He played the solo over and over again until he couldn't breathe anymore. Each time, his mom told him it was his best run-through. Max began to wish he had gotten some tough criticism.

"Why can't I wear a bow tie?" Cole asked with his arms crossed in disappointment.

"Join band when you're old enough, and you can fight with these bow ties too!" Max laughed.

In route to the school, they stopped and picked up Tyler.

His parents had a social function and could not make it to the concert. Max could tell Tyler was bummed out because they wouldn't be there. Max cheered him up by letting him know the family was going for pizza after the concert.

"Think you're ready to blow the audience away with your solo?" Tyler asked Max.

"More like chase them away!" Max joked. "It's going to be a total suck fest!"

"Doubt that, bro. You're the most dedicated one in there." Tyler helped put Max's mind at ease.

As a matter of fact, Tyler had always been the one who could calm Max during the craziest of times. Not long after they first met, Cole had to be rushed to the hospital with a broken leg. Max's parents were out of the house for a while, and Max and Tyler were watching Cole. Max freaked out when Cole fell from a tree he was climbing in the back yard. Tyler forced him to breathe and call his parents. He told Max that broken legs happened every day, but they couldn't be fixed by worry.

When they arrived at the school, they met up with the band and the instructor for one last practice. Everything went smoothly, and their instructor told them it was their best run-through yet. Max smiled with a confidence he hadn't felt in a long time. He knew if his instructor was the one passing out compliments, they must be sincere.

Music had a way of getting into Max's veins and altering his reality. The world could be falling apart, but the perfect song could change that. That feeling was intensified when he was the one making the music. On that stage, all of Max's problems would go away.

The band got through the first song with no problems at all. The crowd cheered, and Max could see Cole jumping up and down in his seat. He loved seeing his little brother's excitement when he played. He was ready to see how excited his brother would be while watching his solo.

The song began as the entire band built up the energy of the next arrangement. Max saw Cole's eyes light up as his solo grew closer. The full band played their final note, and Max jumped in for his moment of glory. A few notes in, the reed of his saxophone broke, and his saxophone squeaked. After a few moments of awkwardness, Max heard the tune of his solo being played on the xylophone. Tyler had picked up where Max left off and saved the show.

Although Max was upset he couldn't finish his solo, he was grateful that Tyler knew the notes. Who knows what would have happened with the song had he not jumped in? Tyler was definitely the MVP of the night. Max couldn't thank him enough.

"I've always got your back! I'm never going to let you fall on your face!" Tyler said.

As his mom was talking to the other parents, Max looked over and saw George, one of the depressed men from the ex-gay group. He must have been a grandparent to one of the band members. Max's heart raced as he headed to the door. He prayed that George wouldn't remember him.

"Hey, fella! Haven't seen you in group!" George stopped Max in his tracks.

Max glanced quickly at Tyler, who was standing right

behind him. "Umm, I've been busy. Sorry, I gotta go!" Max bolted out of the building. Tyler quickly followed behind him.

"What was that all about?" Tyler wondered.

"Oh, it was just a Christian group I went to once. It was super boring!" Max shrugged it off.

Max was relieved when Tyler dropped the subject. The rest of the family made it to the car, and they headed to get pizza. After they were seated, everyone congratulated Tyler for saving the day. Max couldn't help but feel like Tyler was family. Family always had each other's backs.

Tyler decided to spend the night with Max. They stayed up late playing video games and talking about their futures. Max had no clue what he wanted to do other than work with the kids at the church. Tyler wanted to start a band and be their drummer. Max told him they could perform at Max's middle school youth group.

"I want to dedicate a song to my cousin," Tyler said out of nowhere.

"Your cousin? Why?" Max was confused. Could this be what the family emergency was all about?

"He passed away. That's why I was gone. Let's not talk about it." Tyler wiped tears from his face and ended the subject.

Max could feel the hurt that was going through Tyler. He wasn't sure if it was a gift, or a curse, but he often felt the emotions of those around him. He knew Tyler's emotions were much stronger than he was willing to show. It broke Max's heart.

"Hey, I've always got your back. I'm never going to let you fall on your face!" Max repeated the words that Tyler had told him earlier that day.

For the first time, Max saw Tyler really cry. Max went and grabbed some tissues for him. All Max could do was sit there and wait for Tyler to speak up. More than anything, he wanted to hug Tyler, but he didn't want to make Tyler uncomfortable. Like a wall that had fallen down, Tyler began to talk. Tyler reminisced about all of his adventures with his younger cousin, the games of laser tag, bike rides, and basketball one-on-ones that would never be had again.

Chapter 19

Excited and nervous, Max got dressed for the day ahead. Lee was finally going to meet Max's friends, everyone but Tyler of course. Max couldn't help but think about all of the things that could go wrong. What if they didn't get along? Max wasn't sure he would be able to handle the awkwardness if there were any harsh words passed around. He knew that Jess didn't like that Lee kissed him when Lee was a taken man.

"He did what?" Jess had said while walking around a park.

"It was awesome. I felt so close to him! He really wanted to kiss me!" Max defended Lee.

"If he cheated on his boyfriend with you, then he will cheat on you with someone else!" Jess warned.

Max decided to let it go. Deep down, he knew Jess was right, but he couldn't help what his heart longed for. There was no way for him to change his feelings for Lee, just like he couldn't change his attractions towards men.

He made Lee promise to be on his best behavior. Lee was

a bit more edgy, where Max's other friends seemed more at ease. In Max's ideal world, they would all coexist happily. He was well aware that not everything could go his way, but he was sure as hell going to try. He needed this day to go well.

Everyone had agreed on going ice skating. Only Jess and Max had been before. Everyone else was losing their ice skating virginity. It made Max feel good to have the upper hand on Lee. For some reason, Max felt as if Lee was superior to him. It was the one thing Max disliked when hanging out with him.

Any negative thoughts vanished when Lee arrived to pick Max up. Max waved at him to come inside and meet his mom. Thank God his dad was gone. Max was proud to reach the milestone of introducing a guy to his mom. His mom's eyes lit up as she was introduced to the guy who had stolen Max's heart.

"You're just as handsome as Max said you were!" Natalie hugged Lee.

"Thanks Mrs. Stevenson. Your son is a great guy! He speaks very highly of you," Lee responded as if he knew his way to a mother's heart.

"Let's go before she pulls my baby pictures out!" Max grabbed Lee's arms and pulled him towards the door.

"In that case, I want to stay!" Lee shouted, making Max's mom laugh.

"You're good at sucking up!" Max laughed as he jumped into Lee's Jeep.

"That's not all I'm good at sucking!" Lee said, teasingly,

as he blew Max a kiss.

Max's heart melted once again. Lee was probably his biggest source of happiness. Max could not let go of Lee's hand as they drove the fifteen minutes to the ice rink. Honestly, Max wished for more time alone with Lee, but the group was waiting. They got out of the Jeep and made their way into a building that looked more like a warehouse. The metal walls on the outside were getting rusty. Based on its exterior, nobody would be attracted to this place, but the inside said otherwise. Along with the ice rink, there was a gigantic arcade.

"Damn, he is one fine piece of meat!" Lee pointed out a guy putting on ice skates.

"Sorry, he's straight and he's dating one of my best friends. That's Joseph." Max was irritated that Lee was noticing other guy's looks.

Joseph and the girls walked over and introduced themselves to Lee. The way Lee stared at Joseph made Max want to run and hide. How was he supposed to show off his man if Lee wasn't even acting like he was his? Max nudged Lee and told him to knock it off. Max was hoping Joseph didn't notice.

It didn't take five minutes for someone to fall flat on their ass. Joseph's face turned blood red when he saw everyone staring at him. Adrianna began to laugh, although you could tell she didn't mean to. Her laughter was contagious and made its way around to everyone.

"Broken arrow!" Joseph said, laughing. "All of you are going to have to help me learn how to control myself out here!"

Everyone tried to give him advice and verbal support, but Joseph was having no such luck. Lee had caught on so well that he was obnoxiously skating circles around everyone. Adrianna and Jess enjoyed the competition with him. Max was the only one who was willing to buckle down and teach Joseph.

Max hesitantly put his hands on Joseph's waist to keep him balanced. A chill ran up Max's spine when he touched Joseph. Slowly, Max guided him through the motions of a successful ice skater. A slight disappointment settled into Max as he realized Joseph didn't need his hands on his waist any longer. Why did it even matter? Joseph was straight, and Lee was right there with them.

"Your hands felt nice on him, didn't they?" Lee had a sly grin when he asked.

"Maybe I wouldn't have enjoyed it so much if someone else would commit to me!" Max fired back.

"Listen, Max, there is no need to rush into things. Couples that jump right into a heavy relationship don't last. Let's just enjoy our time together." Lee seemed to know what he was talking about.

Max decided he needed to break away from Lee for a second and go talk to the girls. He asked them what their opinion was of Lee, now that they had met him. He really valued their thoughts.

"He seems pretty nice. Sincerer than I would have thought," Adrianna said.

"Honestly, I've been trying hard not to like him, just

because of how you guys met. No matter how hard I try, I can't seem to fully dislike the guy. He has charm," Jess admitted reluctantly.

Max took that as permission from his friends to continue pursuing Lee. Anytime they disagreed with Max, he usually changed his view to match theirs. It was all part of his people pleasing nature. Growing up with a church telling you to put other people first ended up having a negative impact on Max. He sometimes took care of the needs of other people, even if it was at the expense of his own needs.

On one occasion, Adrianna called Max and began to vent about her parents. Max knew he had to be up in the morning for a band concert, but he didn't have the guts to tell Adrianna he had to go to sleep. He stayed up till two in the morning just so she could trash talk her parents. The next morning, he was thirty minutes late to the concert, missing most of the pre-show rehearsal.

Once the cold ice started to get to them, they decided to shop around the mall. Max felt bad because Jess suddenly became the fifth wheel. He didn't have to feel bad long, though. Lee pulled out his phone and said he had to vanish. His mom had texted him, asking him to help around her house. Everyone said goodbye to Lee and continued shopping.

"Now is the perfect time to do this." Joseph pulled out four small bracelets from his pocket.

"What are these for?" Adrianna asked what everyone else was thinking.

"I know I've been obsessed with the whole broken arrow

mentality, but I got us bracelets with arrows on them to remind us that we aren't alone!" Joseph answered proudly.

"They're absolutely beautiful!" Jess raved as she stared at the shiny arrow on her wrist.

"My baby sure knows how to make people happy!" Adrianna winked at Joseph, acting very suggestive.

Max just stared at his bracelet. He began to feel very conflicted. He wanted Tyler to be there with them, but Tyler made the choice to shun him. Max had to push Tyler out of his mind and make the decision to appreciate the friend he had in front of him.

"It's awesome, man! Thanks." Max finally spoke up.

They all hugged goodbye, and Max got into his car. He gripped the steering wheel, as the pain of losing Tyler seeped back in. The hurt felt as excruciating as it had been the day Tyler walked away. Max allowed himself to cry in his car for a few minutes, then he headed back home.

Max stared at the blank screen, wondering what to say. He updated Tyler on how his life was and told Tyler that he missed him greatly. He begged Tyler to tell him why he was so upset. As expected, Max began to tear up again. He looked at the text for a good five minutes before finally hitting send.

Max sat in his bed while staring at his phone, waiting for a buzz. Surely Tyler didn't think Max wanted to make a move on him? Is that why he freaked out and walked away? Max knew that Tyler wasn't religious enough to use faith as an excuse to cease communication.

Suddenly, Max's phone buzzed in his lap. Excited, he

grabbed it and opened the message. His heart sank when he saw the message wasn't from Tyler. However, his mood lifted a little when he saw it was from Joseph, telling him to have a good night. Perhaps it was time to let Tyler go and embrace a new friendship with Joseph.

Chapter 20

Five months before coming out...

It was finally the last day of Max's junior year, and he was more than ready for summer. Pure excitement filled Max's soul when he thought about the summer youth trip he was getting to take with the middle schoolers. Ryan had informed Max that he could take over with the middle schoolers when he started his senior year. Nothing was going to stand in his way.

The timing could not have been more perfect for Max to step up into his new position. Cole would be starting middle school at the exact same time Max took over. Cole seemed ecstatic to hear his brother would be his youth leader. Max felt good, knowing his kid brother looked up to him.

"Can you believe we are going to be seniors next year?" Tyler said while trying to act like a cool kid.

"Watch out Sandersville High!" Max responded sarcastically.

Max, Tyler, Adrianna, and Jess discussed their summer

plans over a nasty, stale school lunch. Tyler's parents wouldn't let him go with Max to help out with the middle schoolers. Instead, he was stuck at home, doing absolutely nothing. Adrianna and Jess were flying to Miami, Florida, with a bunch of other cheerleaders.

"Can I dress like a cheerleader and join you ladies?" Tyler spoke in his best female voice.

"Sisters before misters!" Jess winked at Tyler.

A football player must have heard Tyler joking with the girls because one of them decided to call Tyler a fag. Tyler stood up, his face blood red, and faced the bully. Max wondered why this had to happen on the last day of school, then he realized that there couldn't be much of a punishment if there was no more school.

"You think you can take me?" the asshat asked.

"You bet your ass I can!" Tyler shouted.

Like an angel sent from above, Coach Alan stepped in and told his football player to have a seat. Tyler thanked Coach Alan and wiped the sweat from his brow. His bravery was all an act. Tyler had never been in a fight in his life. He had no intention to start now.

"Man, he almost ruined my perfect face!" Tyler joked as he sat back down with his friends.

The rest of the day went by in a blur. Max was relieved that he would no longer have to see certain attractive students that sent his mind into a confusing whirlwind. There was a guy in chemistry class that had an adorable baby face and long brown hair. You could usually see his six pack through his tight shirt. Also, he would try his best to stop talking to Nick. Max informed Ryan about the Nick situation, and Ryan suggested that they have little to no communication.

Ryan also started monitoring Max's websites with a computer application that would hold Max accountable. Anytime that Max went to a questionable site, Ryan would get a notification. Once, Max forgot about the software and had to have an embarrassing chat with Ryan about his doctor fetish. After that, he no longer used his laptop for porn. Ryan didn't seem to consider the fact that Max's iPhone could do whatever a laptop could.

Thank God, Max thought as the final school bell rang. He cleaned out his locker. It was stuffed to the top with books and old homework assignments. Max had a problem with hoarding papers he didn't need. He tricked himself into believing he would use them to study.

The bus ride home felt like it took forever. Max would try to lay his head against the window, but the vibration of the glass wouldn't let him relax. Max could have sworn there was a faster route than the one the bus driver constantly took. For some reason, Max's parents couldn't pick him up from school that day.

As Max walked up the gravel driveway to his house, he saw a red Chevrolet Cruze. He wondered who was over at his house. Was this why his parents couldn't pick him up? Was it someone who knew Max's secret? Max just knew his secret was out and his life was over. Nervously, he opened the front door and walked inside.

"Surprise!" his family shouted.

Max was startled and nearly had a panic attack. "Wait, are you saying what I think you're saying?"

His dad tossed Max the keys to his new car!

"Congratulations, son. You deserve this car. I'm so beyond proud of you! I also figured it would be a nice chick magnet this summer!"

Max gave a nervous laugh then went in for a family hug. Max wondered if he would still be getting a car if his parents knew about his attractions. Immediately, he pushed that thought out of his head. He was just going to focus on the positive moment that he was living in.

"You guys are squishing me!" Cole yelled from in between the family. Max took that as a sign to give Cole the biggest hug he could, squishing him even more.

"Congratulations to you on finishing elementary school!" Max gave Cole a fist bump. "Where is your car?"

"Very funny! I'm stuck with the bus for a long, long, miserable time!" Cole over-exaggerated the agony.

"How about I take you for a ride?" Max asked Cole while looking at his parents for approval.

After Max got permission, they went out for a joy ride. The feeling of the steering wheel under Max's hands gave him a sense of power. He felt more independent already. He knew he would be able to get Cole to do anything he wanted him to in exchange for a free ride. Max rolled the windows down and let the breeze blow away his worries.

"Can I tell you something?" Cole spoke up through the wind.

"Anything!" Max smiled.

"I don't think I believe there's a God," Cole admitted.

Max wasn't quite prepared for him to drop that bomb. What was he supposed to say to his brother? Cole's mind was still being molded and affected every day. Max didn't want to upset him by arguing against him, but it was important for Cole to believe, right? Max took a few moments to think.

"Why don't you?" Max asked.

"I just don't think it makes sense to me. I'm still going to go to youth group, especially with you teaching, but I'm not convinced," Cole answered, glad he got the news off his chest.

Although Cole was much younger than Max, his bravery and honesty were things that Max admired. For a brief second, Max allowed himself to imagine being honest with people about his attractions. He knew the feelings wouldn't go away, so maybe others should know so that they could help him fight them. Unfortunately, if others knew, Max didn't think he would feel so normal anymore.

Chapter 21

Max and Joseph sat at a coffee shop telling each other their life stories. Joseph could see the dip in Max's mood as he brought up Tyler and the current poor state of their friendship. Max was thankful Joseph was a good listener. It always helped him to vent to somebody. The girls were actually hanging out with Tyler that day, so Max had the day with Joseph.

Lee went to visit some family for a few days, and he wasn't being very talkative. Still, Max cherished every text he got. Max forced himself to understand that Lee had his own life outside of him. He just wished he could be more included in that life. Hopefully in time they would get even closer. Who needs space anyway?

"I'm really sorry things have been so rough for you," Joseph said with real concern in his voice.

"I'm used to it at this point. My life has been one obstacle after another. Honestly, I'm just exhausted," Max said, sighing.

"I have an idea!" Joseph said, suddenly. He immediately got up and started to head towards the door.

"Wait up!" Max called out as he followed behind.

After walking for about five minutes, they arrived at a lone brick building with a rainbow flag hung over the door. Above the flag, it read, *Queer Culture.* Max had no idea this place even existed, but he had a feeling he was going to love it. Joseph said it had all kinds of LGBT merchandise.

"Do you think I'm a dickhead?" Joseph asked as he put on a hat that had a stuffed dick attached to the top.

"Well, people say I'm a pussy!" Max responded, putting on a hat with a vagina on it.

They both spent about an hour in the store, constantly finding fun things to mess with. Max knew Tyler would never do this with him. If you had asked him before coming out, Max would be convinced Tyler would be down for it, but not anymore. He truly thought Tyler was missing out on a lot of fun.

Max found a rainbow headband near the register. He had to have it. As he was checking out, the guy behind the register asked if he and Joseph were a couple. Max laughed and told him that Joseph was straight. Max made a point to express that he had a man. Lee was just hours away at the moment.

On the way out, Max saw a flyer on the store's event board. There was going to be a Gay Pride Party during spring break. Max's eyes widened as he pulled out his phone and texted Lee asking him to go with him. Max was excited to go to his first Pride event. He'd thought about this day, but he wasn't sure his town had much to offer.

"So was that place everything you wanted it to be?"

Joseph asked a clearly pumped up Max.

"Hell yes it was! It made me feel normal!" Max responded.

"You are normal. This thing against LGBT people makes me so mad!" Joseph shook his head.

"You probably wouldn't like my dad!" Max said.

"My uncle is gay, so my dad has no problem with any of it. He says that when he was fighting for America, he was fighting for all people. Including the gay ones." Joseph seemed proud of his dad.

"I never realized how many people weren't straight, until I came out," Max pointed out.

"It'll surprise you. That's for sure." Joseph laughed.

After visiting the store, Joseph invited Max to go on a bike ride. It'd been so long since Max rode a bike, but he was glad to join in. Max was mesmerized by Joseph's house when they pulled in. It was a beautiful, two story home in the back of a fancy neighborhood. It made Max's house look tiny.

Joseph went into the garage and pulled out two red bikes. The boys got on the bikes and started riding down the street. The liberating breeze that hit Max's face reminded him of his first time driving his car. He felt like a bird, free from all the pain of the world below. Then, just like gravity, Lee texted him to tell Max that he couldn't attend the pride party.

"Don't sweat it, man. I'll go with you!" Joseph offered.

"I don't want to make you do that," Max said with a pouty voice.

"Actually, I want to. Plus, my uncle is going to be there.

He's running the tattoo stand. He's a great tattoo artist," Joseph replied.

"You have any tattoos?" Max asked.

Joseph lifted his sleeve to reveal a yin-yang on his upper arm. "I wasn't sure what to get, so I just went with this."

"Hey, I like it. Good choice. Maybe I'll get one!" Max said, joking, knowing his parents would never allow it.

They continued riding their bikes around town. They passed so many nice houses. Max wanted to buy them all. There was an old playground not far from Joseph's house. Max thought it added character to the neighborhood. At one point, Joseph nearly hit a squirrel that was preoccupied by some acorns. Max adored Joseph's worry and concern for the squirrel. Joseph went on and on about how bad he would have felt if he had hit it.

With all of the pretty houses, and Joseph being adorable, Max began fantasizing about buying a house with Joseph. He smiled, thinking about how easily they could coexist together. Max had to force himself to change his thoughts because Joseph wasn't his man. Also, Joseph was into women. More specifically, he was dating one of Max's best friends.

Max couldn't seem to get over the fact that he would not be at the party with Lee, the guy he loved. It felt so wrong, but there was nothing he could do. Max didn't even want to ask Lee why. He didn't want to hear a shitty excuse. He would have to have a good time with Joseph, instead.

Once Max's legs got too tired to keep going, they headed back to Joseph's house. When Max stepped inside, it took his breath away. There was a double staircase covered with beautiful white carpet. Large abstract paintings hung on the walls. A lone grand piano sat right in between the staircases. Joseph gave Max a grand tour of the place. The master bedroom was like something out of a movie. A large canopy bed sat in front of a fireplace. Last, but not least, they got to Joseph's room.

It was a serene deep blue color. Framed poems covered the walls. Max had forgotten that Joseph was a writer. He took his time, reading all of the beautiful words. A few of them even caused his eyes to water. One thing they revealed was that Joseph had a difficult time moving. Max looked over at a picture of Joseph and a group of friends.

"You miss them, don't you?" Max asked, knowing the answer.

"Everyday. I talk to them often, but it's not the same," Joseph said. "People are important, Max. Nobody is meant to be an island."

Max recognized what Joseph said from a sermon he heard before coming out. He knew how true that was, but he also knew letting people in gave them the power to hurt you. Joseph could hurt Max, just like Tyler did. As much as Max knew he needed people in his life, he never wanted to feel the pain of yet again losing a friend. He silently wished that Joseph would never hurt him.

"What inspires you to write?" Max asked, changing the subject.

"A lot of things. People, places, feelings, smells, and any other senses. Once I get started, the words just spill out of me. It's sort of like I'm not even the one writing. Sorry, that was cheesy!" Joseph started laughing.

"No, it's beautiful." Max felt a deep connection with Joseph's poetry. It expressed emotions Max felt in a way he wasn't sure was possible.

"Maybe one day I'll write a little something for you!" Joseph suggested with a smile.

Before long, Joseph's parents got home. Max was introduced as if he was the best friend Joseph had ever had. Even though Joseph's parents were very laid back, their huge, sophisticated home perfectly suited them. They owned a new clothing store that was close to downtown.

"Would you like to stay for dinner?" Joseph's mom, Sarah, asked.

"Sure! I'd love to!" Max's stomach rumbled right on time.

Tim, Joseph's father, showed the boys some of the new clothing designs they got in the store. Max wanted to buy everything he was shown. It explained why Joseph was so stylish all of the time. Max considered stealing some shirts from Joseph's wardrobe. Surely he wouldn't miss anything.

"Max, everyone used to think I was crazy for wanting to design clothes and own my own store. I wouldn't be where I am today if I listened to all of the negative people in my life. Don't listen to that nonsense. You can do whatever you set your mind to!" Tim sounded like a motivational speaker.

"The trouble is, I don't have any clue what I want to do. I do fine in school, and I enjoy my saxophone, but I can't figure out my career path," Max said.

"Don't try to figure it out. Live your life as usual, and let it find you!"

Max thought about Tim's words over dinner. It helped Max to have someone tell him that he didn't have to have his life figured out yet. Whatever he did, he wanted to be able to afford a house like Joseph's family had! Slowly, worry started to creep back in as Max became afraid he would never find a career. What if he never made anything of himself? What if he had nothing to be proud of?

"I have a few extra shirts from dad's store if you want to try them on. They don't fit me anymore," Joseph said.

"Really? I'd love to!" Max wouldn't have to steal any after all.

They had their own little fashion show upstairs with Max being the only model. He let his more feminine side show even though he had tried hard not to reveal that part of himself. He ended up with an abstract shirt with yellow and red patterns and a vibrant pair of pink shorts. Max hadn't had so much fun in quite some time.

Chapter 22

Four months before coming out...

All of Max's bags were packed, and he was ready to head off to the beach. He anxiously paced the entire house until it was time to leave. He was worried that things would go wrong. He was concerned that Ryan would decide that he wasn't fit to lead. He tried telling himself that his fears about being a bad leader were illogical, but it was no use. He would be anxious about it all week.

He played *Halo*, an Xbox game, with Cole to pass time. Even though Max told Cole that he let him win, Cole kicked his ass. Max kept trying to convince himself that it was because Cole had the rocket launcher, but he knew good and well his brother could take him down with any weapon. Angry, Max quit after the second game.

He hugged his family and told them he'd miss them. His dad reiterated how proud he was of him. His mom told him to make sure he had the best time. Cole pouted and told Max to let him sneak on the bus. Max promised Cole that next year would be even better, since he could actually go then.

Max jammed out to his favorite Christian rock songs on the way to the church. He had to be in the zone for the kids. Any impure thoughts had to cease so that he would not be distracted from teaching the youngsters. He was going to be the holiest he could be.

The bus ride was definitely one to remember. The four middle schoolers that he was in charge of kept asking him the most random questions. What's your favorite ice cream? What's your biggest fear? Why is your hair blond? He knew he would have his hands full the whole week.

Finally, the kids' attention shifted to outside the bus. Palm trees were everywhere and behind them was a beautiful beach. Cheers erupted on the bus. Ryan looked at Max and wished him luck. Max laughed, thinking it couldn't be that bad, right?

As soon as they got to the hotel, the kids went straight to the beach. They didn't even put on their swim trunks before getting in the ocean. Max rolled his eyes and watched the boys swim. He couldn't help but feel like one of the boys would drown, and it would be his fault. He didn't want to let these kids down.

After everyone dried off, the group headed to the hotel cafeteria for dinner. Max was amazed at how much the kids could eat. One of them had about thirteen cookies before he started feeling sick. Max knew there was some Bible verse about overeating, he just couldn't think of it in time.

One of the curious boys asked on the way to the convention center for service, "Do you have a girlfriend?"

"No, haven't met anyone yet." Max could sense a lump

in his throat.

Another one piped up, "Are you gay?"

"No!" Max sounded harsher than he wanted to when he answered.

He was thankful that worship gave him an opportunity to calm down. They played some of his favorite songs. He absolutely loved seeing the younger kids worship. In that moment, he wished Cole believed in God. There was such a soothing feeling that came with worship.

The next day, he woke the boys up to head down to the beach. One of the boys did not want to leave the bed. It was probably because he stayed up all night telling random ghost stories. Eventually, Max forced him up and told him to get his trunks on.

"Stop looking at me change, faggot!" the boy said, yelling at one of the other boys who was just minding his own business.

"Excuse me?" Max yelled back. "There is no need for name calling! If you are worried about anyone watching you, go into the bathroom."

"The Bible says fags are bad!"

"It also says to love everyone. Plus, nobody said they were gay! Go change."

Max was shocked that kids that age were capable of such cruelty. It was worse because the boy had used the Bible to fuel his hatred. Max had seen a lot of that, and it confused him. The more Max studied the Bible, the more it didn't make sense. Max vowed his life to God but His word was very controversial. He figured that's why Cole decided not to believe in God. Could he blame him?

Max told Ryan and a few other chaperones about the changing issue. He felt a pain in his heart when one lady blamed the innocent kid by saying he shouldn't be creeping like a pervert. If only she were there and knew what actually had happened. Ryan told him to make sure they behaved. Max was doing his best to keep them in line.

It bothered Max that people were using the Bible as a tool to judge others. The Bible said not to judge, but it was also very harsh towards some people and their life choices. For the first time, he was getting aggravated at religion. He hated seeing the negative effect it could have on the world.

After asking Ryan to keep an eye on his kids, Max decided to take a long walk on the beach. He let the sounds of the waves wash away his stress. The feeling of the sand in-between his toes distracted him from his negative thoughts. He attempted to walk with his feet in the ocean for a while, but the cold water was too much to handle. Before he knew it, he lost sight of the church group, so he decided to head back.

The rest of the week went by much smoother. Max grew to care about his group of boys, and they looked up to him in return. They had so much fun playing in the ocean and building sand castles. The waves were the perfect height, taking the boys under whenever they rolled in. Max's kids even listened well during group devotions. He answered all of their questions the best he could. Most importantly, he let the kids know that they were cared about deeply.

Max did well keeping his kids safe until the jellyfish

incident. One of the boys was flopping around in the surf while Max was putting on some more sunscreen. Suddenly, he heard the boy scream. Panicked, Max ran in and helped the boy out of the ocean. His leg was covered in red lines where the tentacles had wrapped around him.

"Help! Please, it hurts!" the boy said, screaming as tears flowed down his cheeks.

Ryan ran over and asked, "What happened?"

"He's been stung by a jellyfish!" Max said. His heart was racing at this point.

"Pee on him!" another kid suggested.

"God, no!" the boy said.

The lifeguard must have seen the ruckus because he showed up fast with a spray that was meant to take the sting away. The boy cringed as it was applied to the sting. "Thanks for getting me so quickly!" the boy said to Max. Relief quickly followed for him.

Max had to tell himself he couldn't be blamed for what had happened. He felt awful that one of his kids got hurt. Anytime something bad happened around Max, he had a habit of taking on the blame, no matter how little or how much involvement he had. He was just thankful the boy wasn't mad at him.

Before he knew it, Max's week of chaperoning at the beach was over. He began to get a little sad on the way back home. As the kids fell asleep on the bus, he reflected on the past week. He had never experienced something so satisfying as having kids look up to him. It gave him purpose. It fueled him and made him want to be a better person. Still, he had this lingering question on his mind. What would he do if one of the kids told him they were gay?

No matter how hard he tried, Max couldn't convince himself that he would be able to tell them they needed to change their sexuality. The more he learned about the unconditional love of God, the further and further he got from condemning gay people, including himself. In that instant, Max got a strange, yet satisfying feeling when he considered himself gay. He had never let himself be labeled as such.

"I'm gay," he said silently to himself for the first time. The words seemed foreign but like they belonged there all along. Max's muscles didn't seem so tight, and his anxiety faded as he mellowed out. Perhaps this acceptance was the healthiest thing for him.

Max stared out the window and thought about how rapidly his life was evolving. He couldn't help but wonder why his mind had started changing during the youth retreat. It seemed like the last place he would start accepting his sexuality. Maybe it was God telling him it was time to stop fighting and surrender to who he had been this whole time.

"Hey man, great job this week!" Ryan congratulated Max. "I wasn't sure you'd make it through!"

"Thanks! It's been an eye-opening experience!" Max responded, sounding exhausted.

"I'd say so! I wanted to ask you something. I know you've been expecting this, but would you take over with the middle schoolers?" Ryan asked, smiling.

"Oh, wow! You think I did that well?"

"The boys loved spending time with you!"

Max wasn't sure what Ryan would think about his slowly changing mind. Max was questioning and doubting the Bible. Also, he'd begun to judge himself less for being attracted to men. Was he starting to accept himself as a gay man? What would this mean for him as a leader?

Max hesitated before responding, "Of course!"

Chapter 23

Joseph had convinced Adrianna and Jess to join them for the Pride Party. The plan was to meet at A Pizza Paradise before the big celebration. Max put on light blue shorts, a tank top, and his rainbow headband. He looked at himself in the mirror and realized just how far he had come since being a self-hating homophobe. Pride rushed through his veins.

"Have a blast!" his mom called out as he left the house.

"Thanks, Mom!" he shouted back before the door shut.

Max's mom and dad had been going to counseling for a while now. Max wasn't sure if it was working. There was frequent arguing between the two of them. Max did his best to shut it out. If he allowed it to break through his shield, he would surely fall apart. He still blamed himself for their issues.

Max allowed himself to let go of his negative thoughts as he stuffed his face with pepperoni and pineapple pizza. The girls were pretty excited about the party. However, Jess complained that she couldn't hit on any guys because they would all be gay.

"I have a bright idea! Find yourself a nice girl!" Joseph

said, joking.

Jess crossed her arms and responded, "No woman can handle all of this!"

There was a line to get in the outdoor pavilion for the party. As they waited, Max looked at his exciting surroundings. Boys and girls with colored hair, cool piercings, and unique clothing filled the place. Max wished Lee could be there with him. It would've been the perfect way to celebrate their relationship.

Once they bought their tickets, they went in, got some lemonade, and listened to the live band play. They were a mediocre, local rock band called *Queer Chaos*. They screamed on and on about the hardships of being gay. Max wondered if anyone else he knew would see him there. Surely most people knew he was gay, but he didn't tell everyone, so maybe not. Honestly, he could care less. He loved his sexuality.

Everyone decided to go look at the booths that were selling merchandise. Max bought himself a rainbow flag with the fifty bucks his mom had given him. He held onto the rest of the money just in case he found something else. Max smiled from ear to ear when Adrianna and Jess bought shirts that said *Straight but not Narrow.* He was very thankful to have them in his life.

As they were walking, Max heard a couple arguing. He wondered why people couldn't see gays as normal when they argued like any straight couple he knew. He couldn't help but listen in to what they were saying.

"We will leave soon! I just wanted to stop by for a

minute!" said one guy, angrily.

"I told you he is going to be here! I can't be seen with you, so hurry up before I'm caught!" an all too familiar voice shouted back.

Max jerked his head around and saw Lee. His muscles tensed, and his face turned red. Tears welled up in his eyes. A sharp pain developed in his heart. Without realizing what he was doing, he walked up to Lee and decked him in the face. Lee fell to the ground and suddenly every eye was on them.

Lee quickly got back on his feet and charged towards Max. Before he could get to him, Joseph jumped in and tackled Lee to the ground. Whoever Lee was there with took off in fear. Lee fought to get back up, but Joseph held him down.

"Don't even think about hurting my friend! Get the hell out of here, Lee!" Joseph shouted then let Lee get up.

Lee glanced at Max then bolted out of the party. Max ran over to the picnic tables, lay his head down, and cried harder than he had in a long time. Max realized that Lee had lied whenever he said he would leave his boyfriend. All Max could think about was goofing around in the shower with Lee, his first kiss in the car, and dancing to *Gravity*.

The rest of the gang found Max and sat down at the table with him. Max heard Joseph whisper something to the girls about allowing him to cry it out. Max was convinced that he had never been in so much emotional pain in his life, and that was saying something. He had been through a whole lot with accepting himself and coming out.

"I think I want to leave." Max spoke up through the tears.

"If we take you home now, I'm afraid your mood will get worse. We can leave, but I'd like to introduce you to my uncle if you don't mind. He may have some perspective for you," Joseph said.

"Yeah, that's fine," Max replied as he wiped his tears.

Adrianna and Jess told him how sorry they were as they headed towards Joseph's uncle's tattoo stand. Adrianna claimed that she never liked Lee in the first place. Jess promised him that he would find someone. Max thought he already had found the one.

When they made it to the tattoo stand, Joseph introduced everyone to his uncle Clyde. Clyde was an older gentleman, probably in his late fifties, with tattoos all over and pierced ears. He seemed very glad to meet all of Joseph's friends.

"I know Joseph really respects you guys. He needed genuine friends here." Clyde smiled.

"Max here just discovered the guy he liked had been lying to him. Things got ugly. I told him you would have some perspective on hard times," Joseph said, informing his uncle.

"That was you all getting into trouble over there?" Clyde asked. "Well, I've had my fair share of trouble. I was diagnosed years ago with AIDS. I thought it was gonna be the end for me."

"I'm so sorry!" Jess seemed shocked.

"Point is; it wasn't the end. It's no longer a death sentence. With the right medicine, I've been able to live a decent life," Clyde said, ending on a happy note.

"You're probably just emotionally stronger than I am," Max suggested.

"No, what got me through were my friends and family. I started feeling so down about my life recently that my brother had to move into town to help watch over me. That's why Joseph was dragged here," Clyde said. "Having a support system is so important."

"Hey Max, why don't you let my uncle ink you up?" Joseph suggested. "You'll get a good discount."

Max thought about that for a moment. He needed something to lift his spirits, and getting a spontaneous tattoo would definitely do the trick. He knew his father would kill him, but he was eighteen and could do whatever he wanted with his body.

"I'll do it!" Max announced, feeling excited.

Max thought about what kind of tattoo he wanted. It had to have some meaning to him. Max considered what Joseph and Clyde had been stressing to him. He looked down and saw his arrow bracelet, and his idea became complete.

Max wasn't prepared for the sting that came with the ink. It was as if a bee was repeatedly stinging him in his right forearm. He refused to look down at his arm. He wasn't a huge fan of blood. He bit down on the top of his tank top to try and ease the pain.

"We knew he'd be a pillow biter!" Clyde joked.

"What?" Max asked through the pain.

"Just ignore him," Joseph said, grinning.

About forty-five minutes later, Clyde wiped Max's arm down and got off all the blood. Saliva covered the neck of his tank. He had forgotten all about the Lee fiasco during the process of the tattoo. Max was nervous to see what was permanently on his arm, but when he looked down he saw the perfect tattoo. The tattoo showed an arrow, broken in half with the quote, "*We need each other*" around it.

"It's so beautiful!" Jess said. "If I wasn't so afraid of committing to something, I'd get one too!"

"Honestly, I think it's one of the most bad ass tattoos I've seen!" Joseph admitted. "I've seen some pretty good ones, hanging around Clyde."

Max thanked Clyde for the incredible work that had been done on his forearm. He was so pleased with it that he actually began to feel his mood lift. The tattoo gave Max a feeling of power because he had done something for himself even though some people, like his father, would not approve.

In his mind, he played through the many hateful things he wanted to say to Lee. He smiled as he thought about the perfect punch he landed before Lee ran off, chasing after his man. Max wasn't sure if he wanted to contact Lee to let him know how he felt or just drop the whole thing. After all, Lee had stolen a good majority of Max's senior year. Max wasn't sure he was worth spending any more energy on.

"Should I text Lee so I can tell him off?" Max asked for the advice of his friends.

"If you do that, you'll show that he is still getting to you. If you really want to bother him, pretend like he never existed," Joseph suggested.

"Yeah, Joseph is right. Lee clearly wants the attention." Jess said, chiming in.

After considering his friends' advice, Max decided he wanted some closure. He pulled out his phone and went straight to Lee's contact. He clicked edit, then scrolled down to the delete button. His finger paused over the button that would take Lee off of his phone. *Fuck you,* Max thought, as he deleted his contact.

Max saw all of the condoms being passed out at the party, and he realized he would not lose his virginity to Lee, like he had hoped. Max had thought about that day since he met Lee, and now he had to imagine losing it to someone else. He only hoped he would love that person as much as he had once loved Lee.

Once it got dark, fireworks filled the night sky. Max considered that he would not be able to see the beauty of the fireworks without the darkness surrounding them. He figured the darkness in his life was a requirement for him to be able to enjoy the bright moments, as well. However, he wasn't convinced he would be able to handle much more darkness.

Chapter 24

Three months before coming out...

Max was preparing to give his first talk to the middle
schoolers during youth group. The talk was all about God's
unconditional love. He knew it was something he needed to
hear, so he figured it would help the kids, too. It didn't take
long for them to start piling in for service. The boys Max
chaperoned ran up to him and gave him a huge hug. They
were so ecstatic that Max was taking over.

Before it was time for Max to get up and speak, the
church's worship band got on stage and played a few songs.
Something was wrong on this day, though. Max was
struggling to get into worship. He couldn't continue singing
about being fearfully and wonderfully made because he
wasn't honest with everyone about how God made him.
There was some sort of mental block that was preventing
him from getting into his zone.

It didn't take long for Max to identify the feeling. He felt
like a hypocrite going on stage to tell everyone that God
loved them no matter what when he wasn't being honest

about who he was. If God's love was truly unconditional, it shouldn't matter if Max loved other guys. After all, he wasn't hurting a single soul.

Max began to get mad at God for not allowing him to accept himself sooner. He had put himself through a meaningless battle over the past few years. Couldn't God have just told Max that he was fine the way he was? Why would God sit in Heaven and watch so many people struggling with their sexuality?

Max got through his talk just fine. The kids seemed to respond to it well. Afterwards, they played dodgeball until all of the parents had picked their kids up. Max couldn't stop thinking about how Ryan didn't know that his thoughts about homosexuality had changed. He knew he needed to talk to him, but what would the cost be?

After the last kid left, Max found Ryan and asked him to sit down. Max's heart started pumping as his anxiety kicked in. Was he really about to tell Ryan that he thought it might be ok to be gay? He took a deep breath, then he got right to the point.

"I'm thinking that it's ok for me to be gay. God loves me anyway. It's who I am. It's not leaving, no matter how hard I've tried," Max said.

"Oh, well, as your youth leader, it's my job to tell you you're going against the Bible." Ryan seemed deeply concerned.

"The Bible says all kinds of things that we don't follow today," Max replied, defending himself.

"There are multiple passages that condemn that lifestyle.

Please don't do this," Ryan said, pleading with Max to change his mind.

"I'm sorry. I just can't live my life fighting a huge part of who I am. It's already caused enough self-hatred." Max was becoming more firm in his stance.

"I hate to hear this. You're like family. It's probably best you don't talk to the kids anymore. I'll take back over." Ryan's voice got serious.

"Wait, I can't even talk to them? Why?" Max was shocked.

"I'm not sure how the parents would feel about their children being led by an out homosexual. It's nothing against you, Max," Ryan said as he tried to calm Max down.

"Nothing against me? You're treating me like I'm some pedophile! It's not right. I should have never come to you for help!" Max walked out of the building.

Although he expected this consequence, it hurt Max more than he thought it would. When Ryan told him not to speak to the kids, he felt dirty. Ryan made him out to be some kind of freak. That took a massive toll on Max's self-esteem. He needed to pick up his mood. He needed to talk to someone who wouldn't bash him. As he left the church, he picked up his phone and texted Nick.

This time, Max went over to Nick's house. Nick's parents were out, so they went to hang out in his room. Max's senses were immediately overwhelmed by the sheer amount of rainbow-covered items in Nick's bedroom. Secretly, Max was praying that accepting himself as gay didn't mean he'd start acting flamboyant like Nick. He didn't think he would be able to handle himself if he were like that.

"What brings you by, sweet cheeks?" Nick sat down on the bed beside Max.

Max decided to ignore the "sweet cheeks" remark. "Just been doing a lot of thinking. I hate to admit it, but you're right. I'm gay." Shivers went down Max's spine as he spoke the words that he had been fighting to admit for so long.

"Yass! I have been waiting for this day!" Nick stood up and cheered. "Your next step is to come out! That usually starts with the parents. I feel like that's when it's official!"

"I'm not ready for that yet," Max said.

"Are you ready for this?" Nick said as his face went towards Max's.

Max pushed his hand out to stop Nick's attempt to kiss him. Nick told him it was ok as he put his hand on Max's crotch. When Max scooted away, Nick followed. Nick's hands groped Max's junk as Nick tried to get on top of him. Max could barely move.

"Get off of me!"

"Oh come on. I want you so bad." Nick shoved his hand down Max's pants, touching his dick. "See, your reaction means you want it!"

Max pushed Nick off the bed and yelled, "Fuck off!"

Guilt covered Nick's face. He knew what he was doing was wrong, but his hormones had taken over. Max knew that being horny was no excuse. No clearly meant no. He got off the bed and ran out of the house. He felt so unclean. He began to regret admitting he was gay. He knew there was no turning back now, though. It was who he was, no matter how differently other people treated him.

To clear his mind, Max went home to practice the saxophone. As his frustration level rose, he missed more and more notes. When his dad knocked on his door, Max jammed his saxophone back in its case. He would have to practice when he was more relaxed. Tonight was not that night.

"Hey, sport, how was your first day of leading?" His dad had chosen the wrong question.

Max decided to lie. "I can't do it. It's too stressful."

"That's a shame! Cole will be sad," his dad responded, trying to pull the guilt card.

Max really didn't want to upset Cole, so he went to his brother's room to break the news. After a couple of knocks, Cole opened the door. He had dark blue nail polish on that he had gotten from their mom. Max decided to skip right past that and break the news to Cole.

When Max told Cole that he wouldn't be leading, Cole wasn't too destroyed by it. He made Max promise to hang out with him more to make up for it. Cole admitted that he was nervous about middle school. He wanted to have his brother's guidance in some shape or form. He felt as if he wouldn't be able to make friends. He thought he would be an outcast.

"I'm an outcast, and it's not that bad!" Max comforted Cole. "Just be careful about wearing nail polish at school."

"Oh, I'm sorry." Cole put his hands behind his back.

"Just try to love yourself. That's the hardest thing for anyone to do. No matter what, I'll always love you." Max ruffled Cole's hair.

"I just have this feeling everything is going to start changing." Cole let out a huge sigh.

After talking to Cole until his emotions settled down, Max went back into his room. He wrote a few paragraphs in his journal and played some music in the background. He wondered how his brother knew that everything was about to change. They must be more connected than Max ever imagined.

Chapter 25

It was eleven o'clock before Max finally got home. He was a bit worried when he saw the living room lights on. Hesitantly, he opened the front door and stepped inside. He saw his mom sitting in the living room, working on bills. Max knew this was an odd hour to be doing such a thing.

"Hey, you're home. Did you have fun?" Max's mom asked.

"It was very interesting, but yes I did." Max not so subtly revealed his new tattoo.

"Wow! That's really pretty! How are you going to hide that from your father?" she asked.

Max breathed a little easier with her chill response. He was actually pretty surprised that his mom didn't lecture him. He expected at least a little reprimanding from her. After all, he didn't even call to warn her.

"Hide what from me? How was your party?" Max's dad asked while coming down the stairs in his pajamas. He looked aggravated after being woken up by Max coming home.

"It was good. Had fun." Max quickly twisted his arm to

hide the tattoo.

"I'm glad you enjoyed yourself. Now, what's being hidden?" His dad seemed concerned.

Reluctantly, Max showed his father his tattoo. In perfect dad fashion, there was an awkward silence. Max always hated that suspense. Max looked at his mom. She already had her head in her hands, awaiting her husband's response.

"Son, I love you so much. You've been breaking my heart. First, you decide you like boys. Now, you're getting a tattoo. This isn't how I raised you. You used to behave so well!" His dad's voice began to rise noticeably. "I suppose you told him this was ok?" He directed his words towards his wife.

"I had no idea until now, but it's honestly not a huge deal, honey." Natalie stood up for Max.

Max stared, wide eyed, at his mom's boldness. He was so thankful to have a mom who would defend him in the heat of battle. The only problem was that people got hurt in battle. Max waited to see what damage would unfold.

"No big deal? Any time I feel the need to talk sense into our son, you defend him. I'm trying to raise two Christian boys in this house, and you allow them to get away with murder." His dad continued to raise his voice as he gripped the top of the couch.

Max began to get scared as his dad's face turned blood red. Never had Max been terrified of his father. He wondered why his dad was letting things get to him as badly as they were. Apparently, not being able to control his family infuriated his father.

"You are being way too hard on them! Let them choose their own paths. As long as they don't hurt anyone, I don't see the problem!" His mom stood up from the table.

"Of course you don't. You don't know God, so you can't see the truth," his dad said as he shook his head.

"Mom had nothing to do with this. It was my decision! I've tried to live my life to make you happy, but I can't live a lie anymore," Max said, interrupting.

"I'm going to stay at a hotel," his dad announced as he went upstairs to pack his bags.

"I'm so sorry I caused this." Max's eyes welled up with tears as he looked at his mom.

"You didn't cause this. Honestly I figured he wouldn't stay long with the way counseling has been going for us. Maybe this will save our marriage. Only time will tell." Max's mom spoke as if she was relieved.

Max went upstairs and lay in his bed, shocked at what just happened. He was trying so hard to remain positive, but life kept throwing punches at him. He was convinced he wouldn't be able to handle one more blow. Things were just far too heavy. Suddenly, he remembered he didn't have to lift things alone.

Max started a group chat with Joseph, Adrianna, and Jess. They were all pretty shocked about what had happened with his parents. They kept reiterating that they wished they could help, but Max knew of no way they could do that. All they could do was be there to listen to him vent.

A tiny knock came at Max's door. Cole creaked the door open and walked in, wearing Superman pajamas. Max could tell he had been crying. Cole crawled into Max's bed and began crying some more. Before long, the tears were contagious, and they cried together.

"Things are going to be ok." Max was trying to convince himself of the same thing.

"Are they going to split up?" Cole asked through a sniffle.

"Dad's leaving to get some space. This is what they need right now. It may help them out. It's probably not permanent." Max comforted Cole the best he could.

That night, they both fell asleep in Max's bed. The next morning, the boys woke up to the smell of freshly cooked bacon. They quickly made their way downstairs for breakfast. A Sunday without their dad was weird. They were used to seeing him dressed up and ready for church. Even though Max didn't attend church after coming out, he was still used to seeing his dad excited for services.

Most of breakfast was eaten in silence. Nobody wanted to speak up, in fear they would upset someone else. Still, the emotional tension was high. The grip that his mom had on her silverware worried Max. How much longer would it be until she went over the deep end?

"I love your father. I really do! I want you kids to know that." His mom cried while eating her biscuits and gravy.

"We know, Mom." Max reassured her.

"Nothing will change my love for you boys, either." She could barely focus on eating.

Max thought about how his dad was at church, probably hearing about God's unconditional love, while his mom was the one who was showing true unconditional love. The irony made Max laugh. He began to lose a lot of respect for his father. His dad's religious views were making a mess of his relationship with his family. His father chose Christianity because he needed love during a dark time. Yet, he wouldn't show any love during his family's dark time.

Max began to wonder if he would ever go to church again. Was his spiraling faith soon to be obsolete? He began to develop a feeling of hatred towards religion, but he missed the rush he got from worship. Max ached to believe there was something bigger than him that had nothing but love for him.

Max started using the word agnostic to describe himself. His prayers became non-existent. Praying began to seem like a joke to Max. People would say that if God didn't answer a prayer, he had another plan, but Max was convinced it was because there was nobody listening to his prayers. He took off his cross necklace and shut it in his drawer.

Chapter 26

One month before coming out...

As the nights went by, Max could not stop having anxiety over Nick's aggressive actions. He would wake up in the middle of the night, drenched in sweat. He wasn't ready for that type of relationship. Nick was the only one that Max had felt safe talking to, so he knew he had to expand that to more people soon. He couldn't face Nick any longer.

"Dude, it's the start of our senior year, and you've been acting all freaked out. I promise it's going to be a fantastic year." Tyler snapped Max out of his daze during gym class.

It was their first day of class, and they were expected to be active. Coach Alan just wanted them to keep moving the entire period, no matter what that entailed. Max and Tyler decided to run around the basketball court. They weren't the types to play basketball.

"Sorry, it's just been an interesting start to my year," Max responded, running out of breath.

"It's ok. Nobody will make fun of your tiny dick in the shower." Tyler teased Max with a friendly punch on the arm.

Max had totally forgotten that they would have to take group showers today. He promised himself he would try to respect others in the shower, especially Tyler. He knew himself well enough to know that he would probably have a couple of uncontrolled glances at some classmates.

As Max began to take off his gym clothes, panic rushed through his body as he imagined Nick coming onto him. Max had to keep telling himself that moment was over. He took a deep breath and got undressed. Hesitantly, he got in the showers with the other guys. Nobody bothered anyone else, and that helped relax Max.

After school, Max and Tyler hung out in the gym and watched Adrianna and Jess practice cheerleading routines. Tyler talked about how he used to want to date Jess, but her friendship meant too much to him. Max debated telling Tyler about him being gay. He decided he was better off waiting until after he dropped the bomb on his parents.

When the girls were done with cheerleading, everyone went to the mall to hangout. They rarely ever bought anything. They just enjoyed strolling and people watching. The guys at the mall enjoyed watching the girls strut their stuff in their cute cheerleading outfits. It creeped Max out to see guys undress the girls with their eyes, but then he realized he did the same thing to other boys.

They decided they would eat dinner in the food court. Each of them got something different, so they all met up at their favorite table after getting their food. Even when they weren't at school, they felt powerful and entitled because they were finally seniors. Over dinner, they talked about how amazing their year would be.

"If I don't get all A's, I'm going to ask to retake my senior year!" Jess said sarcastically.

"I'll be fine with passing. Nothing wrong with getting D's!" Adrianna responded.

"I'm sure you really love D's!" Tyler fired back, sending everyone but Adrianna into laughter.

"Well, yes, Tyler. I do like dicks! Not sure how that was an insult." Annoyance radiated off Adrianna.

Later that evening, Max and Tyler got together to work on some homework. Tyler asked Max why he wasn't attending church anymore. Max used some bullshit excuse about how busy he was. Tyler had stopped going to church when Max began helping out with the middle schoolers.

"You seemed to have so much fun at the beach though," Tyler pointed out.

Max was irritated that he was pushing a sensitive issue. "I know that. It just wasn't happening for me."

"Dude, chill. I was just curious. I figured it would've been very important to help those kids. They have it rough these days. This world doesn't go easy on them," Tyler responded. "Fuck, I miss my cousin."

Talking about the middle schoolers made Tyler think of his cousin, and once that happened, Tyler shut down. Max felt so bad for him. Nobody deserved to lose someone that young. Max wondered how Tyler's aunt was handling everything. He wished he could take the pain away from his best friend.

Because it was a Friday night, Max stayed over at

Tyler's. They played video games until they couldn't hold their eyes open anymore. Max got into a sleeping bag on the floor, and Tyler got into his bed. They talked about life until Tyler started snoring. Max began to cry when Tyler's snoring turned into sleep talking about his cousin.

Max and Tyler spent their Saturday practicing their instruments. They even wrote their own song. Max's soothing saxophone went well with Tyler's xylophone and random bass hits. Their song seemed to describe their friendship. It was easy going, but it had plenty of strong, confident moments.

They decided one day they would record it. They even wrote down every note on a blank page of sheet music. They didn't necessarily want to make a career with their instruments, but it was the perfect hobby. It helped them grow closer with every note.

"So when we graduate, are we going to throw a huge party?" Tyler stopped playing to ask Max.

"Of course we will!" Max acted as if it was a stupid question.

That night, while Max lay in bed, he knew he couldn't keep his secret for long. He had already lost his church community, so he might as well take the full jump and tell his family and friends. Fall break was coming up, so it would be perfect for him to take time off school and focus on telling his family the truth.

A few weeks later, it was time for Max's eighteenth birthday. His family and friends got together for a fancy dinner at The Cheesecake Factory. It had to be a special occasion for them to splurge on the overly expensive food. As Max looked around the table, he was thankful for everyone there. He couldn't help but smile.

After he devoured his orange chicken, it was time for dessert. When the waitress brought out Max's Oreo cheesecake, it had a single candle lit on top. Everyone began singing the *Happy Birthday* song. Honestly, Max thought they were way too pitchy. When they finished, Max silently wished that life would get better for him after he let the cat out of the bag about his sexuality.

Cole ended up eating a majority of Max's cheesecake. Afterwards, Cole complained about how he was losing his figure. Max wondered where his brother got most of his silly phrases and viewpoints. His dad forced Cole to sit down and stop acting like a woman. That only made Max more nervous about coming out.

A month passed faster than expected. Max was second-guessing his ability to come out to his family. He knew this news would shake them up and affect his whole life. During the drive back home from band practice, Max felt sick to his stomach. He wouldn't be surprised if he threw up in his car while driving.

Max purposely made a few wrong turns so that he could kill time and listen to more of his music. The music helped relax him so that he could face telling his family. He sang along to empowering songs such as *Warrior* by Demi Lovato. With every note, he felt more confident in his decision to come out.

Over and over again, he imagined the many scenarios

that could take place after coming out. If he got kicked out of his house, he would have to go live with Tyler. Maybe his parents would make him go to a conversion camp aimed at changing gay people? There was also a chance none of them would care, but knowing his dad, that was not likely.

Finally, he drove home. After parking, Max sat in his car for a good five minutes. He had gone through so much self-hatred and judgment. He knew once he came out, he could put that behind him and start being happy again, right? It was the only way to move forward. He reached out and grabbed the doorknob, took a deep breath, and walked into his house to set himself on a new path.

Chapter 27

As time went on, Max found it harder and harder to get out of bed. He wasn't convinced there was a point anymore. He had clearly messed everything up for his family, not to mention that he ruined his relationship with his best friend. Max's grades began to reflect his mood. He was barely passing his classes.

He had been so caught up in everything that he had no idea what he was going to do after high school. His first thought was to go to the local college like Joseph, Adrianna, and Jess were, but he wasn't convinced he had the motivation to even start core classes.

As graduation veered closer, Max thought about the party that he and Tyler had discussed. It killed Max that it would never happen. He just wanted to get his diploma and be done with the whole thing. He couldn't share the excitement that everyone else at school had. His heart was too heavy.

His friends noticed the pain he was going through, and they tried to cheer him up. They talked about all of the fun things they would do if Max attended college with them. They raved about the parties, late nights, and visits to bars when they turned twenty-one. Joseph urged Adrianna and Jess to continue talking about the future so that Max could see there was more to life than what he was going through.

Max's mother promised not to tell his dad about his grades as long as he tried to get them up. He wondered how strange graduation would be considering it would be the first time his parents had seen each other since his dad left. All Max could think was that this wasn't supposed to be the way his senior year ended.

Irritability became one of Max's main traits. The smallest inconveniences set him off. He had to apologize over and over again to his friends for flipping out on them for various reasons. His temper was at its worst when they would accidentally bring up Tyler. Max's sadness turned to rage. Tyler had ruined his senior year.

During the final school week, Max decided he wasn't ending the year until he talked to Tyler. Tyler could avoid him at school, but what would he do if Max showed up at his house? He knew it could make things worse, but he didn't care. His life was already falling apart day by day. With two days until graduation, Max drove over to Tyler's.

His heart was beating fast and his chest felt tight as he knocked on the door. He almost backed away and went back home, but he had already made it this far. He needed closure if he was going to move on from their friendship. He took a deep breath as the door opened. Tyler's mother answered the door.

"Max! It's been a while. One moment!" She greeted Max and yelled for Tyler to come downstairs.

Tyler stopped in his tracks when he saw Max. His face turned cold. Max saw Tyler's fists clench. Tyler could stay mad at Max all he wanted, but Max wouldn't leave without knowing why. He couldn't handle wondering why he was so hated anymore.

"What are you doing here?" Tyler asked as he stepped outside and closed the door.

"Stop avoiding me! You were the last person I expected to react poorly to my news. I just want to understand!" Max's body was shaking.

"You really want to know why I can no longer look at you without feeling upset?" Tyler asked, giving Max a chance to back out.

"Yes, I deserve to know!" Max answered.

"You could have been there. If you were honest with me from the beginning, you could have been there for my cousin, and I would not have treated him the way I did!" Tyler spoke as the tears started to flow from his eyes. "My cousin killed himself because he was gay. You pulled me into your world of faith, so all I did was warn my cousin that it wasn't how he was born. I rejected that part of him. Then you come around and say you're out and proud. All I can think of is you and I talking to my cousin and talking him out of killing himself. If I knew you were gay, we could have helped him!"

Max's jaw dropped open. His breathing got heavier as tears began to fall from his face, too. He was paralyzed and speechless. He could have helped a young kid with his sexuality and potentially saved his life. Instead, he hid in the closet like a coward. What was worse was that Tyler blamed him. Without speaking, Max ran to his car and drove off.

Max tried to drive through a full-on panic attack. Between that and the blazing light in his eyes as the sun began to set, he struggled to drive. "I don't want to be alive. I don't want to be alive." Max repeated those six words to himself over and over. Death seemed like the only way to escape the pain he was feeling. He had to make it stop.

Max drove downtown and parked on the side of the street. He walked around, sobbing, until he found a building with a ladder on the side that led to the roof. He used his shaking hands to climb to the top of the building. When he reached the roof, he fell to his knees and began to scream, "Why? Why? Why?"

Max got on his feet and walked to the ledge. A numbing pain took over his body. As he looked down at the road below, he thought about all the hurt he was feeling. He thought about his parents having issues because of him. He thought about Lee lying to his face and breaking his heart. Then, he thought about a young boy's life that he was told he could have saved.

The front half of Max's feet were already over the edge. He kept trying to convince himself to jump. However, there was something nagging him in the back of his mind. He thought about Clyde's optimistic attitude, even after being diagnosed with AIDS. He recalled Clyde and Joseph stressing the importance of having people in your life. Images of Cole finding out Max was dead flashed through his mind. He imagined how devastated his family and friends would be. He almost went over the edge before he fell back.

He quickly pulled out his phone and texted Joseph. The text read, "Broken Arrow!" It didn't take long for Joseph to call. Max answered and tried explaining everything through heavy sobs. "I just don't want to live. I don't want to live. I need help!"

"Where are you, Max?" Joseph asked frantically.

Max explained his location, and Joseph said he was on his way. Max remained on the line, just lying on the top of the building crying. He was unsure how much time had passed when he saw Joseph climbing to the top. Joseph ran over to make sure Max was ok.

"I want to kill myself, Joseph. I really do." Max admitted it once again.

"You're ok. I'm going to get you help. There's a psychiatric hospital a few minutes away that Clyde stayed at. I'll get you checked in," Joseph promised.

After they got in the car, Joseph took Max's phone and called Max's mom. Max could hear his mom freaking out over the phone. He hated himself even more for hurting her like this. He dug his nails into his crossed arms as he lay in a fetal position.

Max began to calm down as Joseph kept repeating, "You're ok. You're ok."

His mom met Max and Joseph at East Ridge Hospital. She rubbed her son's head as they waited for him to be checked in. Luckily, Cole was with his dad, so he didn't have to experience this. Although Max told Joseph he didn't have to stay, he still did. Honestly, Max was beyond thankful that he stayed.

"Max Stevenson!" a nurse shouted from the assessment room.

Max went in and told her his life story and how he wanted to kill himself that night. He still wasn't fully convinced he didn't want to. He informed her that he was just staying alive for his family and friends. Max wished he wanted to stay alive for himself. He wanted life to be enjoyable enough for him to be content with who he was.

It didn't take long for the nurse to decide to admit Max into the hospital. She saw that Max was a clear threat to himself. The nurse went out and spoke to his mother. Max wasn't sure what the nurse was saying, but his mother began to cry. He felt guilty for putting her in this situation. He couldn't imagine what she was feeling.

Before being sent back, Max said goodbye to his mom. She knew that he wouldn't do well without being able to talk to her, so she told him that she would see him on visitation days. She told him that he could call her from the hospital phone whenever he had the chance.

Max wanted his mother to tell his dad because he didn't feel like dealing with it. It would just be another thing for his dad to be disappointed about. She agreed to pass along the news to him, but she advised that Max should also reach out and talk to his father. His mom knew that Max's dad still loved him. Max hugged his mother tight and gave her a kiss on the cheek, assuring her that he would be ok.

"Can I have a second?" Joseph asked before the nurse brought Max back to the unit.

"I know I haven't known you all that long, but you've become one of my best friends here. I've almost been as low as you are now. That was when I first moved and lost most of my friends. Nobody here knew me. Still, nobody here knows that I'm bisexual, except for you now. It's hard to not truly be known. So I can't imagine allowing people to know you and still having to face all this hardship. Anyway, I'm blabbing. I just want you to know that being here doesn't mean you're weak. It means you're strong and you're taking a huge step toward living the life you want to live. You didn't lose tonight. You won. You chose life!" Joseph began getting teary eyed as he hugged Max.

Joseph slipped a sheet of paper into Max's pocket and told him he had written it a few weeks ago. Max thanked Joseph for saving his life, and he gave Joseph another hug. The nurse then told him it was time to go back. Max said one last goodbye.

When he got to the back, they made him pull out his shoe strings. He had to strip down to check for cuts and bruises so that they could monitor if any new marks appeared on his skin. Max felt like he was being judged by the nurses, but he knew that was just his irrational mind talking. Instead of succumbing to negative thoughts, Max chose to dwell on the words Joseph had spoken to him.

That night, Max sat in his hospital bed and looked around his empty room. He found himself grateful he was in there instead of being a pancake on the side of the road. He needed to gain some perspective and learn how to love himself and his life again. However, he wasn't convinced he wouldn't fall apart and want to kill himself once he got back out.

A moment later, a nurse came in to draw blood from Max. The nurse complimented his tattoo as she took the blood. Max refused to look, fearing that he would pass out. When the nurse was finished, she taped some cotton where the needle had been.

"Would you like some medicine to help you sleep tonight?" the nurse offered.

"That would be great. Thank you," Max responded, eager to get some sleep. That night had given him the worst headache.

The nurse came back with a small cup of water and a trazodone. She informed him that it was an antidepressant and a sedative. Max wished she hadn't told him because hearing that he was taking an antidepressant made it all more real to him.

Max stripped down to his underwear and got into the hospital bed. The bed was hard and made an unpleasant noise when Max moved. He wasn't sure how the beds were supposed to be therapeutic. Before long, he started to feel the medication take effect. Drowsiness set in.

Before falling asleep, Max pulled out the paper that Joseph had given him, and read it:

A fragile soul with too much love to hold
Stepping out in the world, with a heart so bold
A gentle smile that lights up the night
A friend so dear, he's worth the fight

I've learned there's more powerful things than blood
Like the people who stay while you're deep in the mud
So I say to you, my friend and my brother
Never forget that we need each other

Epilogue

No one's journey is meant to be taken alone. People need a shoulder to cry on, a hand to hold, and an ear to listen. When rock bottom is staring us in the face, it's other people who can help pull us up and remind us that there is good in the world. Community is what keeps us alive.

Max was on the minds of all of his friends that were graduating on a warm summer day. Even Tyler, shocked to hear the news about him, prayed for Max to find hope as he walked to the stage and grabbed his diploma. He wished he hadn't been so harsh with Max. He just wasn't sure how he could continue a friendship with someone who reminded him of his late cousin. Perhaps time would heal that wound.

Jess imagined what graduation day would be like had Max gone through with his plan, and she thanked whatever higher power there was for keeping Max around. It broke her heart not having Max there to celebrate the end of high school.

Adrianna repeatedly praised Joseph for making sure Max stayed safe. Joseph became the best thing that had ever happened to Adrianna. She felt as if she would be lost without him. She vowed to make sure she would never figure out what life without Joseph was like.

Max's dad wondered where he went wrong with his family. All he wanted to do was guide them on the right path. He realized that with all of the guiding, he forgot to love. He wrestled with how he would love his son who was turning his back away from God. Max's near suicide made his dad realize that he had to make a change for his son's sake.

Max's mom tried to stay strong for her oldest baby. She rarely got any sleep at night thinking about Max in the hospital. The only reason she was thankful for her husband anymore was because he could help take care of Cole while she fell apart. Max's dad moved back in for emotional support. Otherwise, Max's mom may have needed hospitalization as well. Seeing her son reach that low point made her feel like a hopeless failure of a mother.

Cole stayed worried about his brother. He began sleeping in Max's room and pretending like his brother was still there, instead of in the psych hospital. His mom comforted Cole every night, telling him that Max made the courageous decision to stay alive in this sometimes dark world. Cole saw where Max's struggle took him, and he began to wonder, what was he going to do about his difficult, but very different struggle? It was getting to be that time where he could no longer deny it. Cole had his own journey to begin.